Joyce
Marx Machiavelli Chesterton Emerson Austen
Abbott Hardy Montaigne Cooper Hugo
Defoe Melville Haggard Eliot Grimm
Stoker Christie Molière
Carroll Byron Schiller
Wilde Maupassant Engels Smith Kafka
Garnett Einstein Fitzgerald Hawthorne Hall
Goethe Dostoyevsky
Cotton Kipling Doyle Willis
Baum Henry Nietzsche
Leslie Dumas Flaubert Turgenev Balzac
Stockton Vatsyayana Crane
Burroughs Verne
Curtis Tocqueville Gogol Vinci
Homer Widger Tolstoy Whitman Busch
Darwin Thoreau Twain
Potter Freud Zola Lawrence Plato Scott
Kant Jowett Stevenson Dickens Harte
Andersen Burton Hesse
London Descartes Voltaire
Poe Aristotle Wells Cervantes Cooke
Hale James Hastings Irving
Bunner Shakespeare
Richter Chambers
Doré Dante Chekhov Shaw Benedict Alcott
Swift da Wodehouse Pushkin
Newton

Mazelli, and Other Poems

George W. Sands

Imprint

This book is part of TREDITION CLASSICS

Author: George W. Sands
Cover design: Buchgut, Berlin – Germany

Publisher: tredition GmbH, Hamburg - Germany
ISBN: 978-3-8424-4173-6

www.tredition.com
www.tredition.de

MAZELLI, AND OTHER POEMS

By George W. Sands

Contents

PREFACE

Under this head, I desire to say a few words upon three subjects, —my friends, my book, and myself.

My friends, though not legion in number, have been, in their efforts in my behalf, disinterested, sincere, and energetic.

My book: I lay it, as my first offering, at the shrine of my country's fame. "Would it were worthier." While our soldiers are first in every field where they meet our enemies, and while the wisdom of our legislators is justified before all the world, in the perfection of our beloved institutions, our literature languishes. This should not be so; for literature, with its kindred arts, makes the true glory of a nation. We bow in spirit when Greece is named, not alone because she was the mother of heroes and lawgivers, but because her hand rocked the cradle of a literature as enduring as it is beautiful and brilliant, and cherished in their infancy those arts which eventually repaid her nursing care in a rich harvest of immortal renown.

For myself I have little to say. I have not written for fame, and if my life had been a happy one I should never have written at all. As it was, I early came to drink of the bitter cup; and sorrow, whilst it cuts us off from the outer, drives us back upon the inner world;— and then the unquiet demon of ceaseless thought is roused, and the brain becomes "a whirling gulf of phantasy and flame," and we rave and—write! Yes, write! And men read and talk about genius, and, God help them! Often envy its unhappy possessors the fatal gift which lies upon heart and brain like molten lead! Of all who have gained eminence among men as poets, how few are there of whom it may not be justly said, "They have come up through much tribulation."

G. W. S.

Dedication.

Frederick City, September 7th, 1849.

Dear Sir, —

In humble testimony of my gratitude for your services as a friend, and my admiration and respect for your character and worth as an author and a man, permit me to dedicate to you the poem of "Mazelli."

Your obedient servant,

George W. Sands.

To Samuel Tyler, Esq.,

Of the Maryland Bar.

MAZELLI

Canto I. I. "Stay, traveller, stay thy weary steed, The sultry hour of noon is near, Of rest thy way-worn limbs have need, Stay, then, and, taste its sweetness here. The mountain path which thou hast sped Is steep, and difficult to tread, And many a farther step 'twill cost, Ere thou wilt find another host; But if thou scorn'st not humble fare, Such as the pilgrim loves to share,— Not luxury's enfeebling spoil, But bread secured by patient toil— Then lend thine ear to my request, And be the old man's welcome guest. Thou seest yon aged willow tree, In all its summer pomp arrayed, 'Tis near, wend thither, then, with me, My cot is built beneath its shade; And from its roots clear waters burst To cool thy lip, and quench thy thirst:— I love it, and if harm should, come To it, I think that I should weep; 'Tis as a guardian of my home, So faithfully it seems to keep Its watch above the spot where I Have lived so long, and mean to die. Come, pardon me for prating thus, But age, you know, is garrulous; And in life's dim decline, we hold Thrice dear whate'er we loved of old,— The stream upon whose banks we played, The forest through whose shades we strayed, The spot to which from sober truth We stole to dream the dreams of youth, The single star of all Night's zone, Which we have chosen as our own, Each has its haunting memory Of things which never more may be." II. Thus spake an aged man to one Who manhood's race had just begun. His form of manhood's noblest length Was strung with manhood's stoutest strength, And burned within his eagle eye The blaze of tameless energy — Not tameless but untamed—for life Soon breaks the spirit with its strife And they who in their souls have nursed The brightest visions, are the first To learn how Disappointment's blight Strips life of its illusive light; How dreams the heart has dearest held Are ever first to be dispelled; How hope, and power, and love, and fame, Are each an idly sounding name, A phantom, a deceit, a wile, That woos and dazzles to beguile. But time had not yet tutored him, The youth of hardy heart and limb, Who

quickly drew his courser's bit; For though too haughty to
submit, In strife for mastery with men, Yet to a prayer, or a
caress, His soul became all gentleness, — An infant's hand
might lead him then: So answered he, — "In sooth the way My
steed and I have passed to-day, Is of such weary, winding
length, As sorely to have tried our strength, And I will bless
the bread and salt Of him who kindly bids me halt." Then
springing lightly to the ground, His girth and saddle he un-
bound, And turning from the path aside, The steed and
guest, the host and guide, Sought where the old man's friendly door Stood ever open to the poor: The poor — for seldom
came the great, Or rich, the apers of their state, That simple,
rude abode to see, Or claim its hospitality. III. From where
the hermit's cottage stood, Beneath its huge old guardian
tree, The gazer's wand'ring eye might see, Where, in its maze
of field and wood, And stretching many a league away, A
broad and smiling valley lay: — Lay stilly calm, and sweetly
fair, As if Death had not entered there; As if its flowers, so
bright of bloom, Its birds, so gay of song and wing, Would
never lose their soft perfume, Would never, never cease to
sing. Fat flocks were in its glens at rest, Pure waters wan-
dered o'er its breast, The sky was clear, the winds were still,
Rich harvests grew on every hill, The sun in mid-day glory
smiled, And nature slumbered as a child. IV. And now, their
rustic banquet done, And sheltered from the noontide sun By
the old willow's pleasant shade, The guest and host the scene
surveyed; Marked how the mountain's mighty base The valley's course was seen to trace; Marked how its graceful azure
crest Against the sky's blue arch was pressed, And how its
long and rocky chain Was parted suddenly in twain, Where
through a chasm, wide and deep, Potomac's rapid waters
sweep, While rocks that press the mountain's brow, Nod o'er
his waves far, far below;(1) Marked how those waves, in one
broad blaze, Threw back the sun's meridian rays, And, flash-
ing as they rolled along, Seemed all alive with light and song;
Marked how green bower and garden showed Where rose
the husbandman's abode, And how the village walls were
seen To glimmer with a silvery sheen, Such as the Spaniard
saw, of yore, Hang over Tenuchtitlan's walls, When mad-

dened with the lust of gore, He came to desecrate her halls;
To fire her temples, towers, and thrones, And turn her songs
of peace to groans. They gazed, till from the hermit's eye A
tear stole slow and silently; A tear, which Memory's hand
had taken From a deep fountain long congealed; A tear,
which showed how strongly shaken The heart must be,
which thus revealed, Through time's dim shadows, gathering
fast, Its recollections of the past; Then, as a sigh escaped his
breast, Thus spake the hermit to his guest. V. "Thou seest
how fair a scene is here; It seems as if 'twere planned above,
And fashioned from some happier sphere, To be the home of
peace and love. Yet man, too fond of strife, to dwell In meek
contentment's calm repose, Will turn an Eden to a hell, And
triumph in his brother's woes! And passion's lewd and law-
less host, Delight to rave and revel most Where generous Nature stamps and strews Her fairest forms, and brightest hues:
And Discord here has lit her brand, And Hatred nursed her
savage brood, And stern Revenge, with crimson hand, Has
written his foul deeds in blood. But those who loved and suffered then, Have given place to other men: Of all who live, to
me alone The story, of their fate is known; Give heed, and I
will tell it thee, Tho' mournful must the story be. VI. I mind
as if 'twere yesterday, The hour when first I stood beside The
margin of yon rushing tide, And watched its wild waves in
their play; These locks that now are thin and gray, Then clus-
tered thick and dark as thine, And few had strength of arm
like mine. Thou seest how many a furrow now Time's hand
hath ploughed athwart my brow: Well, then it was without a
line;— And I had other treasures too, Of which 'tis useless
now to vaunt; Friends, who were kind, and warm, and true;
A heart, that danger could not daunt; A soul, with wild
dreams wildly stirred; And hope that had not been deferred.
I cannot count how many years Have since gone by, but toil
and tears, And the lone heart's deep agony, I feel have sadly
altered me;— Yet mourn I not the change, for those I loved or
scorned, my friends or foes, Have fallen and faded, one by
one, As time's swift current hurried by, Till I, of all my kith
alone, Am left to wait, and wish to die. VII. How strong a
hand hath Time! Man rears, And names his work immortal;

years Go by. Behold! where dwelt his pride, Stern Desolation's brood abide; The owl within his bower sits, The lone
bat through his chamber flits; Where bounded by the buoy-
ant throng, With measured step, and choral song, The wily
serpent winds along; While the Destroyer stalketh by, And
smiles, as if in mockery. How strong a band hath Time! Love
weaves His wreath of flowers and myrtle leaves, (Methinks
his fittest crown would be A chaplet from the cypress tree;)
With hope his breast is swelling high, And brightly beams
his laughing eye; But soon his hopes are mixed with fears,
And soon his smiles are quenched in tears: Then Disappointment's blighting breath Breathes o'er him, and he
droops to death; While the Destroyer glideth by, And smiles,
as if in mockery. How strong a hand hath Time! Fame wins
The eager youth to her embrace; With tameless ardour he be-
gins, And follows up the bootless race; Ah! bootless—for, as
on he hies, With equal speed the phantom flies, Till youth,
and strength, and vigour gone, He faints, and sinks, and dies
unknown; While the Destroyer passeth by, And smiles, as if
in mockery. Gaze, stranger, on the scene below; 'Tis scarce a
century ago, Since here abode another race, The men of tom-
ahawk and bow, The savage sons of war and chase; Yet
where, ah! where, abide they now? Go search, and see if thou
canst find, One trace which they have left behind, A single
mound, or mossy grave, That holds the ashes of the brave; A
single lettered stone to say That they have lived, and passed
away. Men soon will cease to name their name, Oblivion
soon will quench their fame, And the wild story of their fate,
Will yet be subject of debate, 'Twixt antiquarians sage and
able, Who doubt if it be truth or fable. VIII. I said I minded
well the time, When first beside yon stream I stood; Then one
interminable wood, In its unbounded breadth sublime, And
in its loneliness profound, Spread like a leafy sea around. To
one of foreign land and birth, Nursed 'mid the loveliest
scenes of earth, But now from home and friends exiled, Such
wilderness were doubly wild;— I thought it so, and scarce
could I My tears repress, when standing by The river's brink,
I thought of mine Own native stream, the glorious Rhine!
For, near to it, with loving eye, My mother watched my in-

fancy; Along its banks my childhood strayed, With its strong waves my boyhood played. And I could see, in memory, still My father's cottage on the hill, With green vines trailing round and o'er Wall, roof and casement, porch and door: Yet soon I learned yon stream to bless, And love the wooded wilderness. I could not then have told thee how The change came o'er my heart, but now I know full well the charm that wrought, Into my soul, the spell of thought— Of tender, pensive thought, which made Me love the forest's deepest shade, And listen, with delighted ear, To the low voice of waters near, As gliding, gushing, gurgling by, They utter their sweet minstrelsy. I scarce need give that *charm* a name; Thy heart, I know, hath felt the same,— Ah! where is mind, or heart, or soul, That has not bowed to its control? IX. See, where yon towering, rocky ledge, Hangs jutting o'er the river's edge, There channelled dark, and dull, and deep, The lazy, lagging waters sleep; Thence follow, with thine eagle sight, A double stone's cast to the right, Mark where a white-walled cottage stands, Devised and reared by cunning hands, A stately pile, and fair to see! The chisel's touch, and pencil's trace, Have blent for it a goodly grace; And yet, it much less pleaseth me, Than did the simple rustic cot, Which occupied of yore that spot. For, 'neath its humble shelter, grew The fairest flower that e'er drank dew; A lone exotic of the wood, The fairy of the solitude, Who dwelt amid its loneliness To brighten, beautify, and bless. The summer sky's serenest blue, Would best portray her eye's soft hue; From her white brow were backward rolled Long curls of mingled light and gold; The flush upon her cheek of snow, Had shamed the rose's harsher glow; And haughty love had, haughtier grown, To own her breast his fairest throne. The eye that once behold her, ne'er Could lose her image;—firm and bright, All-beautiful, and pure, and clear, 'Twas stamped upon th' enamoured sight; Unchangeable, for ever fair, Above decay, it lingered there! As it has lingered on mine own, These many years, till it has grown, In its mysterious strength, to be A portion of my soul and me. X. Not in the peopled solitude Of cities, does true love belong; For it is of A thoughtful mood, And thought abides not with the throng. Nor is it won by glittering wealth,

By cunning, nor device of art, Unheralded, by silent stealth, It wins its way into the heart. And once the soul has known its dream, Thenceforth its empire is supreme, For heart, and brain, and soul, and will, Are bowed by its subduing thrill. My love, alas! not born to bless, Had birth in nature's loneliness; And held, at first, as a sweet spell, It grew in strength, till it became A spirit, which I could not quell, — A quenchless — a volcanic flame, Which, without pause, or time of rest, Must burn for ever in my breast. Yet how ecstatically sweet, Was its first soft tumultuous beat! I little thought that beat could be The harbinger of misery; And daily, when the morning beam Dawned earliest on wood and stream, When, from each brake and bush were heard, The hum of bee, and chirp of bird, From these, earth's matin songs, my ear Would turn, a sweeter voice to hear — A voice, whose tones the very air Seemed trembling with delight to bear; From leafy wood, and misty stream, From bush, and brake, and morning beam, Would turn away my wandering eye, A dearer object to descry, Till voice so sweet, and form so bright, Grew part of hearing and of sight. XI. Yet my fond love I never told, But kept it, as the miser keeps, In his rude hut, his hoarded heaps Of gleaming gems, and glittering gold: Gloating in secret o'er the prize, He fears to show to other eyes; And so passed many months away, Till once I heard a comrade say: — "To-morrow brings her bridal day; Mazelli leaves the greenwood bower, Where she has grown its fairest flower, To bless, with her bright, sunny smile, A stranger from a distant isle, Whom love has lured across the sea, O'er hill and glen, through wood and wild, Far from his lordly home, to be Lord of the forest's fairest child." It was as when a thunder peal Bursts, crashing from a cloudless sky, It caused my brain and heart to reel And throb, with speechless agony: Yet, when wild Passion's trance was o'er, And Thought resumed her sway once more, I breathed a prayer that she might be Saved from the pangs that tortured me; That her young heart might never prove The sting of unrequited love. My task I then again began, But ah! how much an altered man, — A single hour, a few hot tears, Had done the wasting work of years. XII. Nor was it I alone, to whom Those words had been as words of doom, By some malicious fiend rehearsed: Another one was standing by, With princely port, and piercing eye, Of dusky cheek, and brow, and plume; I thought his heaving heart would burst, His labouring bosom's heave and swell, So strongly, quickly, rose and fell! A long, bright blade hung at his side, Its keen and glittering edge he tried; He bore a bow, and this he drew, To see if still its spring were true; But other sign could none be caught, Of what he suffered, felt, or thought. And then with firm and haughty stride, He turned away, and left my side; I watched him, as with rapid tread, Along the river's marge he sped, Till the still twilight's gathering gloom Hid haughty form, and waving plume.

Canto II.

I. He stood where the mountain moss outspread Its smoothness beneath his dusky foot; The chestnut boughs above his head, Hung motionless and mute. There came not a voice from the wooded hill, Nor a sound from the shadowy glen, Save the plaintive song of the whip-poor-will,(2) And the waterfall's dash, and now and then, The night-bird's mournful cry. Deep silence hung round him; the misty light Of the young moon silvered the brow of Night, Whose quiet spirit had flung her spell O'er the valley's depth, and the mountain's height, And breathed on the air, till its gentle swell Arose on the ear like some loved one's call; And the wide blue sky spread over all Its starry canopy. And he seemed as the spirit of some chief, Whose grave could not give him rest; So deep was the settled hue of grief, On his manly front impressed: Yet his lips were compressed with a proud disdain, And his port was erect and high, Like the lips of a martyr who mocks at pain, As the port of a hero who scorns to fly, When his men have failed in fight; Who rather a thousand deaths would die, Than his fame should suffer blight. II. And who by kith, and who by name, Is he, that lone, yet haughty one? By his high brow, and eye of flame, I guess him old Ottalli's son. Ottalli! whose proud name was here In other times, a sound of fear! The fleet of foot, and strong of hand, Chief of his tribe, lord of the land, The forest child, of mind and soul Too wild and free to brook control! In chase was none so swift as he, In battle none so brave and strong; To friends, all love and constancy,— But we to those who wrought him wrong! His arm would wage avenging strife, With bow, and spear, and bloody knife, Till he had taught his foes to feel, How true his aim, how keen his steel. Now others hold the sway he held,— His day and power have passed away; His goodly forests all are felled, And songs of mirth rise, clear and gay, Chaunted by youthful voices, where His battle-hymn once filled the air— Where blazed the lurid council fire, The village church erects its spire; And where the mystic war-dance rang, With its confused, discordant clang, While stern, fierce lips, with many a cry For blood and vengeance, filled the sky, Mild Mercy, gentle as the dove, Proclaims her rule of peace and love. And of his true and faithful clan, Of child and matron, maid and man, Of all he loved, survives but one— His earliest, and his only son! That son's sole heritage his fame, His strength, his likeness, and his name. III. And thus from varying year to year, The youthful chief has lingered here; Chief!—why is he so nobly named? How many warriors at his call, By Arcouski's breath inflamed, Would with him fight, and for him fall? Of all his father's warrior throng, Remains not one whose lip could now Rehearse with him the battle song, Whose hand could bend the hostile bow. And yet, no weak, complaining word, From his stern lip is ever heard; And his bright eye, so black and clear, Is never moistened by a tear; Of quiet mien, and mournful mood, He lives, a stoic of the wood; Gliding about from place to place, With noiseless step, and steady pace, Haunting each fountain, glen, and grot, Like the lone Genius of the spot. IV. And this was he who, standing there, Seemed as an image of Despair, Which agony's convulsive strife, Had quickened into breathing life. The writhing lip, the brow all wet With Pain's cold, clammy, deathlike sweat; The hand, that with unconscious clasp, Strained his keen dagger in its grasp; The eye, that lightened with the blaze Of frenzied Passion's maniac gaze; The nervous, shuddering thrill, which came At intervals along his frame; The tremulously heaving breast, — These signs the inward storm confessed: Yet, through those signs of wo, there broke Flashes of fearless thought, which spoke A soul within, whose haughty will Would wrestle with immortal ill, And only quit the strife, when fate Its being should annihilate. Silent he stood, until the breeze Bore from his lips some words like these. V. "The words I speak are no complaint And if I breathe out my despair, It is not that my heart grows faint, Or shrinks from what 'tis doomed to bear. Though every sorrow which may shake Or rend man's heart, should pierce my own, Their strength united, should not make My lip breathe one complaining tone. If I must suffer, it shall be With a firm heart, a soul elate, A wordless scorn, which silently Shall mock the stern decrees of fate. The weak might bend, the timid shrink, Until misfortune's storm blew by, But I, a chieftain's son, should drink Its proffered cup without a sigh. And it will scarcely, to my lip, Seem harsher than yon fountain's flow, For I have held companionship With Misery, from my youth till now — Have felt, by turns, each pang, each care, Her hapless sons are doomed, to bear; — I caught my mother's parting breath, When passed she to the spirit land; And from the fatal field of death, Where, leading on his fearless band, With fiery and resistless might, He fell, though victor in the fight, Pierced by the arrow of some foe, I saw my father's spirit go. And I have seen his warrior men, From mountain, valley, hill, and glen, Departing one by one, since then, As from the dry and withered spray, The wilted leaves are blown away, Upon some windy autumn day: I, only I, am left to be The last leaf of the blighted tree, Which the first wind that through the sky Goes carelessly careering by, Will, in its wild, unheeded mirth, Rend from its hold, and dash to earth: Thus, here alone have I remained, An outcast, where I should have reigned. VI. "How shall I to myself alone, The weakness of my bosom own? Why, mindful of my fame and pride, When my brave brethren had died; Why, with my friendly, ready knife, Drew I not forth my useless life? Was it a coward fear of death,

That bade me treasure up my breath? Or had life yet some genial ray, That wooed me in its warmth to stay? Had earth yet one whose smile could stir, My spirit with deep love for her? Yes, though within me hope was dead, And wild Ambition's dreams were fled; Though o'er my blighted heart, Despair Desponded, love still nestled there; Love! how the pale-faced scorner's lip Would sneer, to hear me name that name; Yet was it deep within my soul A secret but consuming flame; Whose overruling mastership, Defied slow Reason's dull control! And felt for one of that vile race, To whom my tribe had given place; Was nursed in silence and in shame! Shame, for the weakness of a heart, Yet bleeding from th' oppressor's blow, Which could bestow its better part Upon the offspring of a foe! They, the mean delvers of the soil, The wielders of the felling axe,— Because we will not stoop to toil, Nor to its burdens bond our backs; Because we scorn Seduction's wiles, Her lying words and forged smiles, They, the foul slaves of lust and gold, Say that our blood and hearts are cold.(3) But ere the morrow's dawning light Has climbed yon eastern craggy height, One, whose fierce eye and haughty brow, Are lit with pride and pleasure now, Shall learn, at point of my true steel, How much the Red man's heart may feel,— How fearlessly he strikes the foe, When love and vengeance prompt the blow! Though scorned by him, I know an art Could stop the beatings of his heart, Ere his own lips could say, 'Be still!' A single arrow from my bow, Bathed in the poisonous manchenille,(4) Would in an instant lay him low; So deadly is the icy chill, With which the life-blood it congeals, The wounded warrior scarcely feels Its fatal touch ere he expire: But, when Revenge would glut his ire, He stops not with immediate death The current of his victim's breath; With gasp, and intervening pause, The lifeblood from its source he draws, Marks, in the crimson stream that flows, How near life verges to its close,— And its last soul-exhaling groan, To him is music's sweetest tone! And he, whose fate it is to die, Ere Morning's banner flouts the sky, The eye shall see, the arm shall know, That guides and deals th' avenging blow; And ere his spirit goes to rest, Right well his scornful heart shall learn, How fiercely, in a savage breast, The flames of love and hate may burn." He spake, and down the mountain's side, With quick, impatient step, he hied, Threading the forest's lonely gloom, A ruthless minister of doom. VII. 'Twas midnight; calmly slept the Earth, And the mysterious eyes above, Gazed down with chastened looks of love, Not, as when first they hymned her birth, With ardent songs of holy mirth, But mournfully serene and clear; — As on some erring one we gaze, Whose feet have strayed from wisdom's ways, But who, in error, still is dear. Far o'er yon swiftly flowing stream Fair fell the young moon's silver beam, And gazing on its restless sheen, Stood one whose garb, and port, and mien, Bespoke him of a foreign land, One born to win, and hold command; The master mind, the leading one, Where deeds of manly might were done. Yet, by the hallowed glow, that came O'er lip and cheek, o'er eye and brow, He who beheld, might guess that now His thoughts were not of wealth and fame: Whence could that veiling radiance shine, Save from Affection's holy shrine? And this was he, who from afar, Had come to bear away his bride; And love had been the guiding star, That lit him o'er the trackless tide; "To-morrow, on its sunny wing, My bridal hour soon shall bring; And those bright orbs which o'er me shed Such gentle radiance from on high, Shall shine upon my nuptial bed, When next they walk along the sky. O! what are all the pomps of earth, Of honour, glory, greatness, worth, Beside the bliss which Love confers Upon his humblest followers!" He said, and from the river turned; — An eye, that with fierce hatred burned, Met his, and this reply was made: "Thou, haughty one, shalt be a shade Ere dawns the coming morrow's sun." Then, ere the point he could evade, He felt the sharp steel pierce his breast, While he, who the foul deed had done Stood calmly by, and saw him sink In death, beside the water's brink, Saw, gush by gush, the crimson blood Pour out, and mingle with the flood; Then drew his dagger from its rest, And gazing on its fearful hue, Said, "Thou hast yet one task to do. He who, death-wounded, welters there, Came hither, o'er the deep to bear Far off from her paternal nest, The white dove I have watched so long. The falcon's wing was bold and strong, Yet thou hast stayed him in his flight; Strike one more blow, and thou to-night May'st rest;" then laid his bosom bare, And buried deep the dagger there, And by his victim's lifeless trunk, Without a sigh or groan he sunk.

Canto III.

I. With plumes to which the dewdrops cling, Wide waves the morn her golden wing; With countless variegated beams The empurpled orient glows and gleams; A gorgeous mass of crimson clouds The mountain's soaring summit shrouds; Along the wave the blue mist creeps, The towering forest trees are stirred By the low wind that o'er them sweeps, And with the matin song of bird, The hum of early bee is heard, Hailing with his shrill, tiny horn, The coming of the bright-eyed morn; And, with the day-beam's earliest dawn, Her couch the fair Mazelli quits, And gaily, fleetly as a fawn, Along the wildwood paths she flits, Hieing from leafy bower to bower, Culling from each its bud and flower, Of brightest hue and sweetest breath, To weave them in her bridal wreath. Now, pausing in her way, to hear The lay of some wild warbler near, Repaying him, in mocking tone, With music sweeter than his own; Now, o'er some crystal stream low bending, Her image in its waves to see, With its sweet, gurgled music blending, A song of tenfold melody; Now, chasing the gay butterfly, That o'er her pathway passed her by, With grace as careless, glee as wild, As though she were some thoughtless child; Now, seated on some wayside stone, With time's green, messy veil o'ergrown, In silent thoughtfulness, she seems To hold communion with her heart, Beguiling fancy with the dreams That from its Pure recesses start. II. There is a silent power, that o'er Our bosoms wields a wizard might, Restoring bygone years to light, With the same vivid glow they wore, Ere time had o'er their features cast The shadowy shroud that veils the past: — To those who walk in wisdom's way, 'Tis welcome as an angel's smile; But those who from her counsels stray, Whose hearts are full of craft and guile, To them 'tis as a constant goad — A weight that doubles Sorrow's load, — A silent searcher of the breast, Which will not let the guilty rest. In childhood's pleasant season born, It haunts us in all after time; From youth's serene and sunny morn To manhood's stern meridian prime. From manhood, till the weight of years, And life's dull constant toil, and tears, And passion's ever raging storm, Have dimmed the eye and bowed the form. True, youth, of hope and love possessed, By friends — youth has no foes — caressed, Finds in the present — happy boy! — Enough of gaiety and joy; And man, whose visionary brain Begets that idle phantom train Of shadows — Power, Wealth, and Fame, — A scourge — a bubble — and a name — So often and so vainly sought — Has little time for peaceful thought; And so they turn not back to gaze, Where faithful memory displays Her record of departed days; But oh! how loves the eye of age, To move along its pictured page, To scan and number, o'er and o'er, The joys that may return no more; The hopes that, blighted in their bloom, By disappointment's chilly gloom, Were given sadly to the tomb; The loves so wildly once enjoyed, By time's unsparing hand destroyed; The bright imaginative dreams, Portrayed by restless fancy's beams, By restless fancy's beams portrayed, Alas! but to delude and fade! To count these o'er and o'er again Is age's sole resort from pain. Then, stranger, marvel not that I Have claimed so long thy listening ear; I could not pass in silence by Themes to my memory so dear, As those which make my story's close — Mazelli's love, Mazelli's woes. III. Ascending from the golden east, The sun had gained his zenith height, The guests were gathered to the feast, Prepared to grace the marriage rite; The youthful and the old were there, The rustic swain and bashful fair; The aged, reverend and gray, Yet hale, and garrulous, and gay, Each told, to while the time away, Some tale of his own wedding day; The youthful, timorous and shy, Spoke less with lip than tell-tale eye, That, in its stolen glances, sends The language Love best, comprehends. The noontide hour goes by, and yet The bridegroom tarries — why? and where? Sure he could not his vows forget, When she who loves him is so fair! And then his honour, faith, and pride, Had bound him to a meaner bride, If once his promise had been given; But she, so pure, so far above The common forms of earthly mould, So like the incarnate shapes of love, Conceived, and born, and nursed in heaven, His love for her could ne'er grow cold! And yet he comes not. Half way now, From where, at his meridian height, He pours his fullest, warmest light, To where, at eve, in his decline, The day-god sinks into the brine, When his diurnal task is done, Descends his ever burning throne, And still the bridegroom is not, there— Say, why yet tarries he, and where? IV. Within an arbour, rudely reared, But to the maiden's heart endeared By every tie that binds the heart, By hope's, and love's, and memory's art,— For it was here he first poured out In words, the love she could not doubt,— Mazelli silent sits apart. Did ever dreaming devotee, Whose restless fancy, fond and warm, Shapes out the bright ideal form To which he meekly bends the knee, Conceive of aught so fair as she? The holiest seraph of the sphere Most holy, if by chance led here, Might drink such light from those soft eyes, That he would hold them far more dear Than all the treasures of the skies. Yet o'er her bright and beauteous brow Shade after shade is passing now, Like clouds across the pale moon glancing, As thought on rapid thought advancing, Thrills through the maiden's trembling breast, Not doubting, and yet not at rest. Not doubting! Man may turn away And scoff at shrines, where yesterday He knelt, in earnest faith, to pray, And wealth may lose its charm for him, And fame's alluring star grow dim, Devotion, avarice, glory, all The pageantries of earth may pall; But love is of a higher birth Than these, the earth-born things of earth,— A spark from the eternal flame, Like it, eternally the same, It is not subject to the breath Of chance or change, of life or death. And so doubt has no power to blight Its bloom, or quench its deathless light,— A deathless light, a peerless bloom, That beams and glows beyond the tomb! Go tell the trusting devotee, His worship is idolatry; Say to the searcher after gold, The prize he seeks is dull and cold; Assure the toiler after fame, That, won, 'tis but a worthless name, A mocking shade, a phantasy,— And they, perchance, may list to thee; But say not to the trusting maid, Her love is scorned, her faith betrayed, — As soon thy words may lull the gale, As gain her credence to the tale! And still the bridegroom is not there — Oh! why yet tarries he, and where? V. It was the holy vesper hour, The time for rest, and peace, and prayer, When falls the dew, and folds the flower Its petals, delicate and fair, Against the chilly evening air; And yet the bridegroom was not there. The guests, who lingered through the day, Had glided, one by one, away, And then, with pale and pensive ray, The moon began to climb the sky, As from the forest, dim and green, A small and silent band was seen Emerging slow and solemnly; With cautious step, and measured tread, They moved as those who bear the dead; And by no lip a word was spoke, Nor other sound the silence broke, Save when, low, musical, and clear, The voice of waters passing near, Was softly wafted to the ear, And the cool, fanning twilight breeze, That lightly shook the forest trees, And crept from leaf to trembling leaf, Sighed, like to one oppressed with grief. Why move they with such cautious care? What precious burden do they bear? Hush, questioner! the dead are there; — The victim of revenge and hate, Of fierce Ottali's fiery pride, With that stern minister of fate, As cold and lifeless by his side. VI. Still onward, solemnly and slow, And speaking not a word, they go, Till pausing in their way before Mazelli's quiet cottage door, They gently lay their burden down. Whence comes that shriek of wild despair That rises wildly on the air? Whose is the arm so fondly thrown Around the cold, unconscious clay, That cannot its caress repay? Such wordless wo was in that cry, Such pain, such hopeless agony, No soul, excluded from the sky, Whom unrelenting justice hath Condemned to bear the second death, E'er breathed upon the troubled gale A wilder or a sadder wail; — It rose, all other sounds above, The dirge of peace, and hope, and love! VII. And day on weary day went by, And like the drooping autumn leaf, She faded slow and silently, In her deep, uncomplaining grief; For, sick of life's vacuity, She neither sought nor wished relief. And daily from her cheek, the glow Departed, and her virgin brow Was curtained with a mournful gloom, — A shade prophetic, of the

tomb; And her clear eyes, so blue and bright, Shot forth a
keen, unearthly light, As if the soul that in them lay, Were
weary of its garb of clay, And prayed to pass from earth
away; Nor was that prayer vain, for ere The frozen monarch
of the year, Had blighted, with his icy breath, A single bud in
summer's wreath, They shrouded her, and made her grave,
And laid her down at Lodolph's side; And by the wide Potomac's wave, Repose the bridegroom and the bride. 'Tis
said, that, oft at summer midnight, there, When all is hushed
and voiceless, and the air, Sweet, soothing minstrel of the
viewless hand, Swells rippling through the aged trees, that
stand With their broad boughs above the wave depending,
With the low gurgle of the waters blending The rustle of their
foliage, a light boat, Bearing two shadowy forms, is seen to
float Adown the stream, without or oar or sail, To break the
wave, or catch the driving gale; Smoothly and steadily its
course is steered, Until the shadow of yon cliff is neared, And
then, as if some barrier, hid below The river's breast, had
caught its gliding prow, Awhile, uncertain, o'er its watery
bed, It hangs, then vanishes, and in its stead, A wan, pale
light burns dimly o'er the wave That rolls and ripples by
Mazelli's grave.

Notes To Mazelli

Note 1.

"And how its long and rocky chain Was parted suddenly in
twain, Where through a chasm, wide and deep, Potomac's
rapid waters sweep, While rocks that press the mountain's
brow Nod O'er his waves far, far below."

"The passage of the Potomac, through the Blue Ridge, is perhaps,
one of the most stupendous scenes in nature. You stand on a very
high point of land. On your right comes up the Shenandoah, having

ranged along the foot of the mountain a hundred miles to seek a vent. On your left approaches the Potomac, seeking a vent also. In the moment of their junction, they rush together against the mountain, rend it asunder, and pass off to the sea.

"The first glance at this scene hurries our senses into the opinion that this earth has been created in time; that the mountains were formed first; that the rivers began to flow afterwards; that, in this place particularly, they have been dammed up by the Blue Ridge Mountains, and have formed an ocean which filled the whole valley; that, continuing to rise, they have at length broken over at this spot, and have torn the mountain down from its summit to its base.

"The piles of reckon each hand, but particularly on the Shenandoah, the evident marks of their disrupture and avulsion from their beds by the most powerful agents of nature, corroborate the impression. But the distant finishing which nature has given to this picture, is of a very different character. It is a true contrast to the foreground. It is as Placid and delightful as that is wild and tremendous.

"For, the mountain being cloven asunder, she presents to the eye, through the cleft, a small catch of smooth blue horizon, at an infinite distance in the plain country, inviting you, as it were, from the riot and tumult roaring around, to pass through the breach, and participate of the calm below." — Jefferson's Notes on Virginia.

Note 2.

"Save the plaintive song of the whip-poor-will."

That the Indian mind and language are not devoid of poetry, the names they have given to this bird (the whip-poor-will) sufficiently evidence. Some call it the "Muckawis," others the "Wish-ton-wish," signifying "the voice of a sigh," and "the plaint for the lost." Those, who in its native glens at twilight, have listened to its indescribably melancholy song, will know how beautifully appropriate these names are.

Note 3.

"They, the foul slaves' of lust and gold, Say that our blood
and hearts are cold."

It has been advanced by some writers, that the almost miraculous
fortitude often displayed by Indians, under the most intense suffering, is to be accounted for by their insensibility to pain, resulting,
they allege, from a defective nervous organization. From the ab-
sence of a display of gallantry and tenderness between the sexes,
they argue also, in them, the nonexistence of love, and its kindred
passions. This we think unjust, as it robs them of the honours of a
system of education, which is life-long, and whose sole object is to
attain the mastery of all feeling, physical or mental. The view taken
of this subject by Robertson, in his History of America, to us, seems
most accordant with truth. He says: "The amazing steadiness with
which the Americans endure the most exquisite torments, has in-
duced some authors to suppose that, from the peculiar feebleness of
their frame, their sensibility is not so acute as that of other people;
as women, and persons of a relaxed habit, are observed to be robust
men, whose nerves are more firmly braced. But the constitution of
the Americans is not so different in its texture, from that of the rest
of the human species, as to account for this diversity in their behav-
iour. It flows from a principle of honour, instilled early and culti-
vated with such care, as to inspire him in his rudest state with a
heroic magnanimity, to which philosophy hath endeavoured in vain
to form him, when more highly improved and polished. This invin-
cible constancy he has been taught to consider as the chief distinc-
tion of a man, and the highest attainment of a warrior. The ideas
which influence his conduct, and the passions which take possession of his heart, are few. They operate of course with more decisive
effect, than when the mind is crowded with a multiplicity of objects,
or distracted by the variety of its pursuits; and when every motive
that acts with any force in forming the sentiments of a savage,
prompts him to suffer with dignity, he will bear what might seem
impossible for human patience to sustain. But whenever the fortitude of the Americans is not roused to exertion by their ideas of
honour, their feelings of pain are the same with those of the rest of
mankind."

Note 4.

"Bathed in the poisonous manchenille."

The slightest wound from an arrow dipped in the juice of the Manchenille, causes certain and speedy death. "If they only pierce the skin, the blood fixes and congeals in a moment, and the strongest animal falls motionless to the ground." — Robertson's America.

S. L. Sawtelle.

Dear Sir:

To you, who have given me friendship in adversity, counsel in perplexity, and hope in despondency, permit me, as an expression of my deep and lasting gratitude, to inscribe the "Misanthrope."

With sentiments of the highest respect,

Your obt. servt.,

George W. Sands.

Frederick City, September 1849.

> Dramatis Personae. Werner — Misanthrope. Manuel — a cottager. Albert — his son. Rebecca — wife to Manuel. Rose — his daughter. Spirits. An aerial chorus.

THE MISANTHROPE RECLAIMED

A Dramatic Poem

ACT I.

A fountain near the summit of a mountain, from which, through a deep glen, a stream descends to the valley below. A city seen in the distance. Time, midnight. Werner standing near the fountain. Werner (solus). Eternal rocks and hills! Mighty and vast; and you, ye giant oaks, Whose massy branches have for centuries Played with the breeze and battled with the storm, He, who so oft has trod your rugged paths, And laid him down beneath your shades to rest, Returns to be your dweller once again. I sooner far would make your wilds my home, With nought but your rude eaves to shield me from The winter's cold or summer's heat, than be One of the hundred thousand human flies That swarm within yon filthy city's walls. Here, I at least may live in solitude, Free from a forced communion with a race, Whose presence makes me feel that I am bound, By nature, to the thing I loathe the most, Earth's stateliest, proudest, meanest reptile, man! The beauty of a god adorns his form, The foulness of a fiend is in his heart; The viper's, or the scorpion's filthy nest Nurses a far less deadly, poisonous brood Than are the hellish lusts, the avarice, — The pride — the hate — the double-faced deceits — That make his breast their dwelling. If he be not beneath hell's wish to damn, Too lost for even fiends to meddle with, How must they laugh to hear him, in his pride, Baptize his vices, virtues; making use Of holy names to designate his crimes; Giving his lust the sacred name of love; Calling his avarice a goodly sin, Care for his household; naming his deceit Praiseworthy caution; boasting of his hate, When he no more can cloak it, as a proof Of strength of mind and honesty of heart. For all of goodness that remains on earth, The name of virtue might be banished from it. Fathers, who waste in shameful riotings The bread for which their children cry at home; Mothers, who put aside th' unconscious babe That they may wrong its father; children, who Grow old in crime ere they have spent their youth; These are its habitants. I cannot brook the thought, that I belong To their vile race. My sufferings have been great, And keen enough to prove my immortality; For dust could not have borne what I have suffered. My mind has pierced far, far beyond the length Of mortal vision, and discovered things Of which men scarcely dream, and paid in pain, The price of what it learned and bought with pangs By which a thousand ages were compressed Into one hour of agony: a power Which is a terror to possess, and yet This one thought only irks me. Methinks the peaceful earth will scarcely give My dust a resting-place within its bosom, But cast it forth as if too vile, to mingle With clay that ne'er has been the slave of sin. What! other watchers here at this lone hour? [An evil spirit enters, singing. The world is half hidden, By midnight's dark shadow; The filly, witch-ridden, Skims over the meadow; The house-dog is barking, The night-owl is hooting, The glow-worm is sparkling, The meteor is shooting; And forms, which lie So stiff and still, In their shrouds so chill, Through the live-long day, Now burst their clay, And flit through the sky, On their dusky pinions: Hell's dominions Keep holiday. Sisters, sisters, wherever your watches Are kept, fleet hither to me, Fleet hither, fleet hither, and leave earth's wretches Alone to their misery. [A chorus of evil spirits answer as they enter from different parts of the mountain. We come! Vice needs no assistance, She meets no resistance, Virtue's existence Is only in name; Drinking and eating, Intriguing and cheating, Carousing, completing Their ruin and shame; Old age unrepenting, Manhood unrelenting, Youth sighing and winning, Deceiving and sinning, Deserting, repining, All men are the same. Ho! ho! Earth quakes with the weight of the anguish she bears, Her plains and her valleys are deluged with tears, And her sighs, if united, were deeper by far, Than the thunderbolt's peal, when the clouds are at war. There is, not a bosom, that bears not within Its chambers, the blot and the burden of sin; Not a mind, but in many an hour bath felt The curse of its nature, the pangs of its guilt. These earth-worms! whose sire would have had us to bow To his dust-moulded Godship! what — what are they now? In the scale of true goodness, they sink far below The poor, patient ox, that they yoke to the plough. Let them revel awhile, in the false glaring light Of deception, that blindness but seems to make bright; Let them gather awhile of time's perishing flowers; The revenge of eternity! This shall be ours! Ho! ho! [They settle near the fountain. The first Spirit addresses them. The night is advancing, Come, let us, dancing In dewy circles deftly tread; And while we dance round, New schemes shall be found, To ruin the living, and trouble the dead. [They form a circle on the margin of the stream, and dance round singing. I. Life is but a fleeting day, Half of which man dreams away; Night! we follow in thy train— Sleep! supreme o'er thee we reign; Ours the dreams that come when thou Sit'st upon the unconscious brow; Reason then deserts her throne, We then reign, and we alone. II. Then seek we, for the maiden's pillow, Far beyond the Atlantic's billow, Love's apple, and when we have found it, Draw the magic circle round it;(1) Fearless pluck it, then no charm That it bears may do us harm; Place it near the sleeper's head, It will bring love's visions nigh, And when the pleasing, dreams are fled, The waking, pensive maid will sigh, Till her bosom has possessed, The form that made her dreams so blest. And when a maiden finds a lover, Her happy days are nearly over: Nature hath unchaste desires, Love awakes her slumbering fires, And the bosom that is true in Love is ever near its ruin; Passion's pleading melts the frost Of chilliest hearts, and all is lost: For, once vice blots a maiden's name, She soon forgets her maiden shame. III. Haunt the debauchee with dreams, Of the victim of his schemes; Paint her with dishevelled hair, Streaming eyes, and bosom bare, And with aspect pale and sad, As a spectre's from the dead, Weeping o'er her new-born, child, Her name reproached, her fame despoiled: Let her groanings reach his ear, Pierce his heart, and rouse his fear Of the retribution given, To such deeds as his, by Heaven. IV. Around the drunkard's tattered couch, Let pale-faced want and misery crouch, His children shivering o'er the hearth, Cheered by no sound of social mirth, Upbraiding, with their timid glances, The author of their sad mischances; And she to whom the holy vow Of the altar bound him, now With sunken eye, and beauty faded, Tresses silvered, brow o'ershaded, Clinging to him fondly still, With a love that mocks each ill, Which would vainly strive to tear Her soul from one who once was dear. Now haste we, each our task to do, Ere the starry hours wane through! [They fly off, singing as they disappear. Ere the Morning's rosy wing, Has brushed the damp night-shades away, Ere the birds their matins sing, Choiring to the new-born day, Though its bright birth-hour be near, Many a sigh, and many a tear, Shall attest the mystic might, Of those who walk the world by night. Werner (solus). The ruin of the living! if that be Your only task, you have a poor employ. Give man his three score years, and he will make A wreck, the skill of hell might show forth as A sample of its handiwork, and then, Exult at the completeness of its ruin. The troubling of the dead! — if memory lives In that far world, to which the spirit hastens, When she casts off the clay that clogs her wings, E'en there ye are forestalled, for man will need No curse, to make his second life a hell, If be retains the memory of his first. Had the clear waters of this gurgling brook, The pow'r to wash time's blots from th' mind's page, And all earth's mountains were compact of gold, Her rivers nectar, and her oceans wine, Her hills all fruitful, and her valleys fresh, And full of loveliness as Eden was, Ere sin's sad blight fell on its living bow'rs, And all were mine, I'd give them but to lay My weary limbs along this streamlet's bed, And sleep in full forgetfulness awhile. But, I forget my task — now let me to it! [He takes a vial from his bosom, and flings its contents into the air, chanting, Spirit Wherever be thy home, In earth or air, My message hear, And fear it. By the power which I have earned, To which thy knee has knelt, By the spell which I have learned, A spell which thou, hast felt, I bid thee hither come! [A white cloud appears in the distance, floating up the glen, and a voice is heard, singing as it approaches, I. I saw from port a vessel steer, The skies were clear, the winds were fair, More swiftly than the hunted deer, Upon her snowy wings of air, She flew along the silv'ry water, As fearlessly as if some sprite, Familiar with the deep, had taught her, A spell by which to rule the might Of winds and waves, when met to try Their strength, up midway in the sky. II. Along her trackless watery way, With unabated speed she flew, Still gay and careless, till the day Waned past: night came: the heavens grew Black, dread and threat'ning. Then the storm Came forth in its devouring wrath; Before it fled Fear's pallid form; Destruction followed in its path; It passed: the morning came: in vain, I look for that lost bark again. III.

Far down beneath the deep blue waves, Within some merman's coral hall, Her fated crew have found their graves; Above them, for their burial pall, The mermaids spread their flowing tresses; The waters chant their requiem; From many an eyelid, Pity presses Her tender, dewy tears for them: The natives of the ocean weep, To view them sleeping death's pale sleep. IV. Thou, mortal, wast the bark I saw; The waters, were the sea of life; And thou, alas! too well dost know, What storms were imaged in the strife Of winds and waves. The hopes of youth, Thou, in that bark's lost crew, may'st see, — All buried now within that smooth, Vast, boundless deep, — eternity: — And I, a spirit though I be, Can pity still, and weep for thee. [The cloud settles near the fountain, and, un-closing, discovers a beautiful form looking steadily at Werner. WERNER (addressing it). How beautiful! If intercourse between all living worlds, Had not been barr'd by Him who gave them life, I should believe thou wert the guardian spirit, Of that which men have named the Queen of Night. Like her, thou art majestic, pale and sad, And of a tender beauty: those bright curls That press thy brow, and cling about thy neck, Seem made of sunbeams, caught upon their way To earth, by some creative hand, and woven Into a fairy web, of light and life, Conscious of its high source, and proud to be A part of aught so beautiful as thou. I have seen many full, bright mortal eyes, That were a labyrinth of witching charms, In which the heart of him who looked was lost; But none like thine; their light is not of earth; Their loveliness not like what man calls lovely. Beside the smoothness of thy brow and cheek, The lily's lip were rough; each of thy limbs, Is, in itself, a being and a beauty. If that the orb thou didst inhabit, ere Thou wert a portion of eternity, Was worthy of such dwellers, oh! how fair And glorious, must have been its fields and bow'rs! How clear its streams! how pure and fresh its airs! How mellow were its fruits! how bright its flow'rs! How strong and brave the beings, fit to share It with thee! 'Tis most strange that He, whose hand Fashions such wondrous things, should take delight In striking them to nothingness again! Perchance the author of all evil had Invaded it, and made it quite unfit To be a part of God's great universe. And yet thou lookest as if thou wert beyond The power of temptation to assail. Hast thou too sinned? Spirit. I have lived as thou livest, died as thou Wilt have to die, and am what thou shalt be. Werner I have not questioned thee of life or death, Nor of the state which shall succeed them both; I care not for the first, nor fear the second; The last I leave to Him who gave to man Eternity for his inheritance. But I would know if the unceasing war, Which good and evil wage upon the earth, Has reached beyond, its confines. Spirit. Have I not answered thee? The Begetter of worlds, stars, suns, and systems! The Father of Creation! the Bridegroom Of the Spirit! hath He not written that Death has dominion only over sin? And thou would'st know if other worlds have felt The curse that fell upon, and blighted thine. Poor simple child of clay! no doubt thou know'st The story of the Eden of thy sire, And think'st that there, in its fresh, stainless breast, The baleful seeds of evil first were sown, Which since have spread so fearfully abroad,— When the sad doom, that came on him and his, Was but the spray, cast from the wave of fate, Which just then reached thy newly finished orb. Where it first started— whither tends its course— Where it shall stop—how many wrecks of worlds— Once fairer far than thine was at its birth— Shall strew its desolate way,—is not for things Brought forth from dust to know. What wouldst thou of me? Werner. The sole remaining good, if good it be, That yet is mine to share. I have tried all That earthly hope holds out to satisfy The longings of man's nature. I have loved, And made an idol of the thing I loved, And worshipped it with all my soul's intensity; And, for awhile, the frenzy of my dream Shut out all other thoughts. But it was short; Death plucked my lovely flower from my grasp, And then, the icy chill of desolation Came, like a snowy avalanche, upon My heart, and froze the fountains of its feeling. I was ambitious. I have striven for, And worn, the gaudiest wreath of fame, and when I would have placed it on my brow, it grew A mountain in its weight. I courted much The notice of the world, and when men praised, The very breath that bore their praise to me, Seemed clogged with pestilence. Wealth, too, I coveted, And heaped its shining dust in hoards around me, And yet it was but dust, as barren of Enjoyment as the ground we tread upon. I clad myself in purple—heaped my board With all the fairest, sweetest fruits of earth, And filled my golden goblets with bright juice, Pressed from the goodliest grapes, and made my couch Of down, and yet, I was most wretched still. My garments were but cumbersome; my couch Could give no rest, and e'en my generous wines Could not remove the crushing weight that sat, Nightmare-like, on my heart, until it grew A palpable and keenly aching pang. There is, one path which yet remains untrod; To be my guide in it, I called thee hither,— 'Tis that of knowledge. Spirit. The same In which the mother of thy race was lost, With e'en a wiser, mightier guide than I. She thirsted, too, for knowledge, and she gave Her innocence—her home in Paradise— The happiness of him—who shared her lot— To know—what? That her own rebellious hand Had raised the flood-gates of a sea of crime, Which would for ever pour its bitter waves Upon the helpless unprotected race, Which her rash deed had ruined. Think of the sighs—the groans—the floods of tears— The woes—too deep for these—which have no end, Save but in heart-breaks! Think upon the toil— The sweat—the pain— the strife—the crime—the blood— The myriads of souls with which this one Sad lesson was obtained! whose price is yet Not fully paid, nor shall be so, until The last poor son of earth mingles with dust! Dost thou not fear to tread a path like this? Werner. I have no fear; It is so long since I have felt its thrill That 'twere a pleasure now to feel it. Spirit. What wouldst thou know? Thou art familiar with all earthly lore. More: Thou hast gained, and wield'st a power, to which The rulers of the elements do bow; The hurricane, at thy command goes forth, Walking where'er thou bid'st it, and the storm Ceases to howl when thou hast said,—"Be still!" Thine anger stirs the ocean, and thy wrath Finds out the deep foundations of the mountains, And shakes them with its strength; the subtle fire, That lights the tempest on its gloomy way, Starts from its cloud-rocked slumber, at thy call, To be thy messenger. Canst thou not be content when thou art feared By those who rule a world? What is there yet Which thy insatiate mind desires to know? Would'st learn immortal mysteries? Reflect Thou art but mortal. Werner. Spirit, why dost thou Taunt me with my mortality? "Weak things, Brought forth from earth," — "Poor simple child of clay," — These are thy words, when well thou knows't that I, Though bound to earth by bonds made of its mire, Am mightier than thou. Were it not so, Thou would'st not now be face to face with one Of mortal birth. Thou, too, canst feel revenge, And knowest how to wreak it; but, take heed, — The power which brought thee hither, can, and may Deal harshly with thee. If thou knowest aught Worthy of an immortal mind to know, To which I have not pierced, reveal thy knowledge. Spirit. We may not tell the secrets of eternity; But I can show thee things thou hast not seen, And they may profit thee, although 'twill shake Even thy proud heart to look upon them. Would'st see them? Werner. It is my wish. Spirit. Come then. Werner. Lead on; Although thy path be through hell's gloomy gate, I too will pass its portals at thy back. Thou canst not enter where I dare not pass. [The cloud closes around them, and moves away, and a voice sings as it disappears. To the region of shadow, The region of death, Where dust is a stranger, And life has no breath; Where darkness and silence Their dim shrouds have cast Round the phantoms of worlds That belong to the past; Spirits who sit on The thrones of the air, Guide ye our chariot, Waft ye us there. [Exeunt.

ACT II.

The verge of Creation. Enter Werner and Spirit. Werner. We have outtravelled light and sound: The harmonies that pealed around us, as Through yon array of dim and distant worlds We winged our flight, have wholly died away, Or come to us so faintly echoed, that Our ears must watch and wait to catch them. Those stars are now like watch-fires, which though seen Blazing afar, send not their light to make The path of the benighted wanderer More plain and cheerful.

Before us stretches one vast field of gloom, So dense as to appear impenetrable:— Darkness, that has a body and a form, Both palpable to touch and sight, across Our path a barrier rears that seems to bar Our farther progress. If there be, beyond This wall of blackness, aught of mystery, What power shall guide us to it? Spirit. Thy mind Which, from the influence of matter, free As it is now and shall be till again Though art returned unto thy native orb, Is its own master, and its will is now Its only needed guide. Strange things are hidden by that ebon veil, To which a single wish of thine may bear us. Werner. Then let us on: Since we our search for knowledge have begun, Wherever there is aught that Power has made, Which Time has ruined, or which Fate has damned, There let us go, that we may look on it, And learn its history. What intense glooms We now are passing through! I feel them part Before, and close behind us, as we fly, As plainly as the swimmer feels the waves That lave his gliding limbs. This sure must be The home of Death—no voice, no sound, no sigh, Not ev'n so much of breath as would suffice To make a lily tremble! Spirt. Though say'st true, This is indeed the realm of Death,—at least It has no more of life than what though hast Brought here with thee,— I speak of mortal life: We now are near the Hades of past worlds, Whose spirits have a life which cannot die. You laugh! and show the haughty arrogance Which in your mortal brethren you cotemn. Think you that he who gave to man his mind, The undying spark that quickens his clay frame, Would fashion from the same material Such mighty wonders as the spheres which go Hymning around his everlasting throne! Giving to them a beauty which alone Could be conceived by him, which has great hand Alone could mould into reality, And yet deny them what he gave to thee, Intelligence! a thing that knows not death? Hast though not seen thine earth put forth her leaves, Clothing her rugged mountain tops and sides, Her forests in the vale, each tree and shrub, With a fair foliage? hast though not beheld Her weaving, in the sunny springtide hours, A fairy web of emerald-bladed grass To robe her valleys in? With every flow'r Of graceful form, and soft and downy leaf, And tender hue, and tint, that

Beauty owns, To deck her gentle breast? When Autumn came, With its rich gifts of pleasant, mellow fruits, Hast though not seen her wipe her sunburnt brow, And shake her yellow locks from every hill? Hast though not heard her holy songs of peace And plenty warbled from each vocal grove, And murmured by her myriads of streams? Hast though not seen her, when the hollow winds, Which moan the requiem of the dying year, Raved through her leafless bowers, wrap about Her breast a mantle, wherewith to protect And nurse the seed, the trusting husbandman Hath given to her keeping? Are thine acts As full of wisdom, and as free from blame? If not, then why deny to her the life And spirit you possess? Werner. I did not laugh In disbelief of what thy words declare, But they stir such strange thoughts within my mind, That, as I will not weep, I can but smile. Methinks the darkness has grown less profound, — A heavy, dim, and shadowy light, like that Which, when the storm has chosen midnight's hour Of stilly gloom, to hold its revel in, First glimmers through the clouds which have been rent, And torn by their own fierceness, hands about us. The light increases still, and in the distance, Enormous shadows, wearing distinct shapes, Since seemingly immovable, and others Like mighty, mastless, sailless, vessels, moved By magic o'er a tideless, waveless ocean, In calm, majestic silence float along! Spirit. Let us go nearer, Now what seest though? Werner. Worlds like to that I live on, save that these Seem made of living shades instead of dust; Vast mountains, with tall trees and mighty rocks, And fountains, gushing from their very summits; Huge, towering cliffs, and deep and lonely glens, And wide-mouthed caves that hold a deeper gloom, — With precipices from whose edges soft And silvery cataracts are leaping down; Swift streams, that rush adown their rugged sides, And quiet lakelets, that appear to sleep In the embrace of the surrounding hills; The cottage of the hardy hunter, perched High on the rocks, like to an eagle's nest: The shepherd's humble shieling, and his fold, And, half-way up, broad vineyards, with their vines Bending with purple clusters of ripe fruit; — Wide valleys, with green meadows, and pure streams, And gentle hills, where ripening harvests stand; Majestic rivers, with their verdant banks Studded with towns, and rural villages; Motionless lakes, and seas without a wave, And oceans pulseless as a dead man's heart! And mighty cities, standing on their coasts, With vasty walls and gilded palaces, And giant tow'rs, and tapering spires, that seem The guardians of all they overlook. Churchyards, with their pale gravestones, that appear Like watchers of the dead whose names they bear! All these are there, but not a sign of life, No living thing that creeps along the ground, Or flies the air, or swims the wave, is seen. It seems as if on all things some strong spell Had in the twinkling of a star came down And rocked them to an everlasting sleep! Spirit! tell me if what I see is more Than a delusion; if it be, whence came These shades? Spirit. And have I not already said That these things are, that they are quick with life, — Such life as disembodied spirits have, — That they are deathless? Thou need'st not inquire Of me whence they are come, for thou hast seen One of their number on its journey hither. The period may not be far remote When thine own planet, starting from its sphere, Shall fright the dwellers of the stars that skirt Its destined pathway to these silent realms! Thou'st seen the comet rushing through the sky, And, gazing on the glowing track which it Had branded on the azure breast of space, Thinking thy words were wisdom, thou hast said, "When its full term of years has been fulfilled, It shall return again." Not knowing that The light thou sawest was reflected from That sacred fire, which, in the end, shall purge The spirit essence which pervades creation, From the dull dust with which a wayward fate Has clogged its being! Question me no more — Remember what I said — I dare not tell The secrets of Eternity. Look on And learn whate'er thou canst. Werner. There is one thing which I at last have learned, — To feel that with the increase of our knowledge Our sorrows must increase. I oft have heard, But never before have felt the truth of this. To know that were it not for this clay mask, I even now might pierce the shadowy veil That wraps in mystery the things I see, And comprehend their secret principle, Will make life doubly hard to bear, and tempt Me much to shake it prematurely off, And snatch wings for my spirit ere its time. A total ignorance were better than The flash which from its slumber wakes the mind, And then, departing, leaves it to itself, In the wide maze of error, darkly groping. Wisdom is not the medicine to heal A discontented mind. I now know more Than when I left the earth, but feel that I Have bought my knowledge with increase of sorrow. Spirit. Did I not tell thee that its path were steep, And hard to climb, and thick beset with thorns,— And that its tempting, longed-for fruit, tho' bought With a great price, is full of bitterness? If though art satisfied, let us retrace Our way to earth again; wert thou to go Yet farther on, thou might'st regret the more Our coming hither. Werner. What! is there aught still more remote than these From the great centre of the universe,— The fair domain of life and living things? Spirit. There is,— A kingdom tenanted with such dark shapes, That angels shudder when they look on them! Thou surely dost not wish to visit it. Werner. Why not? There is within my mind a void Whose vacant weight is harder to be borne Than the keen stingings of more active pangs; When it has traced the mystic chain of being To its last link, it may perchance shake off The misery of restless discontent,— Its fulness then may sink it into rest. Spirit. I have no power to disobey thy word; If thou wilt on, I must proceed with thee, Even though in looking on I share the pangs Of those who suffer. Werner. Come, then, I too must see them, tho' it cost Me years of pain to gaze but for a moment. Spirit. 'Twere harder now to find Eve's' buried dust, Than to declare who has inherited The largest portion of her prying spirit. (Sings.) Where Pain keepeth vigil With Sorrow and Care, And Horror sits watching By dull-eyed Despair,— Where the Spirit accurst Maketh moan in its wo, Thy wishes direct us, And thither we go. [Exeunt.

ACT III.

Scene I. Near the place of the damned. Enter Werner and Spirit. Werner. What piercing, stunning sounds assail my ear! Wild shrieks and wrathful curses, groans and prayers, A chaos of all cries! making the space Through which they penetrate to flutter like The heart of a trapped hare,—are revelling round us. Unlike the gloomy realm we just have quitted, Silent and solemn, all is restless here, All wears the ashy hue of agony. Above us bends a black and starless vault, Which ever echoes back the fearful voices That rise from the abodes of wo beneath. Around us grim-browed desolation broods, While, far below, a sea of pale gray clouds, Like to an ocean tempest beaten, boils. Whither shall we direct our journey now? Spirit. Right down through yon abyss of boiling clouds, If though hast courage to attempt the plunge, Our pathless way must be. A moment more And we shall stand where angels seldom stand, And devils almost pity when they stand,— Behold! Werner. Eternal God! Whose being, is of love, whose band is pow'r, Whose breath is life, whose noblest attribute,— The one most worthy of thyself~-is mercy! Were these of thine immortal will conceived? Has thy hand shaped them out the forms they wear? Has thy breath made them quick with, breathing life? And is thy mercy to their wailings deaf? Poor creatures! I bad deemed that in my breast Grief had congealed the hidden fount of tears, But ye have drawn them from their frozen source And I do weep for you! Spirit. What moves thee thus? I thought thy heart so steeled in hardihood Of universal hate, and pride, and scorn, That even were the woes, which thou dost here Behold endured by others, heaped on thee, Thy haughty soul unmoved would feel them all; Accounting its development of strength To bear the worst decrees of ruthless fate, Sufficient recompense! Werner. Misdeem me not, If I have wept involuntary tears O'er pangs beyond my pow'r to mitigate, Believe me, 'twas in pity, not in fear. But tell me, Spirit! is all hope extinct In those who here sojourn, or do they look Yet forward to some blest millennial day, Which shall redeem them from this horrid place. Spirit. Best ask your theologians that question. Some say that there are places purgatorial, Where Error pays the price of her transgressions In sufferings that efface the effects of sin. And other some declare that when the soul And clay are parted, heaven seals the doom Of both, beyond repeal. Let thy own mind Sit arbiter 'twixt these, and choose the truth. Mark what approaches us, and mark it well. Werner. I cannot turn my gaze from it, and yet It makes the warm blood curdle in my veins. Than it, hell cannot hold a fouler form — A thing of more unholy loathsomeness! Its heavy eyes are dim and bleared with blood, Its jaws, by strong convulsions fiercely worked, Are clogged and clotted with mixed gore and foam! A nauseous stench its filthy shape exhales, And through its heaving bosom you may mark The constant preying of a quenchless flame That gnaws its heartstrings! while a harsh quick moan Of mingled wrath, and madness, and despair, Perpetually issues from its lips; — And with unequal but unceasing steps, It chases through the hot, sulphureous gloom, A mocking phantom, — fair as it is foul! With naked arms, white breast, and ebon locks, And big black eyes that dart the humid flame Which sets the heart ablaze; and red moist lips, And checks as spotless as the falling flake Ere it has touched the earth, and supple form Wherein is knit each grace of womanhood In its perfection! and with wanton looks That speak the burning language of desire, It seems to woo its loathsome follower, — Yet ever from his foul embraces flies. And on his brow his name is written, "Lust!" Dismiss the spectre, for it blasts my sight, And sears my brain with its dark hideousness! Spirit. 'Tis gone; look up and see what next appears. Werner. A frame which may be that of Hercules, It hath such giant members! and its port Is martial as e'er marked a Caesar's moving. Its sandals are of brass, its massive brow Is helmeted in steel, and in its hand It bears a sword with which, in idle strokes, It vainly beats the unresisting air, As if in battle with some phantom foe; And at each blow it deals, a strong fatality Turns back its sword's keen point on its own breast, Which deep it gashes, — then in mournful tone, It mutters o'er and o'er again these words, — "I fought for fame and won unending wo." His agonies seem like himself, immortal. Spirit. Justice is blameless of his sufferings: For many years his busy, plotting brain, Made discord out of union, strife from peace, And set the nations warring till the earth Was crimson with the blood poured out for him! He bears what he inflicted,— let him pass And mark what follows him. Werner. A goodly shape, More fit to string and strike Apollo's lyre, Than bear the shield or wield the sword of Mars! A broken harp, suspended at his side, A faded garland, wreathed about his brow, Tell what he was, and still employ his care. With thin white hand, that trembles at its task, In vain he strives to bind the broken chords, And to their primal melody attune them;— In vain,—for to his efforts still replies A boding strain of harsh, discordant sound. And then, with hot tears coursing down his cheeks, He lifts his faded wreath from his pale brow, And gazing on its withered leaves, exclaims,— "For earthly fame I sung the songs of earth, Forgetful of all higher, holier themes,— 'Tis meet the meed I won should perish thus." Is not the justice which confines him here Akin to cruelty? for his sad heart Seems, as his earthly strains were, full of softness. Spirit. Each thought, and word, and deed of mortal man, Is but a moral seed, which, in due season, Must bring forth fruit according to its kind. The soil wherein those seeds are sown is Time,— Death is the reaper of the ripened harvest,— The fruits are garnered in Eternity, To be, or good or bad, the spirit's food! If then our thoughts, and words, and deeds have been Of corrupt tendency, or evil nature,— What marvel if we feed on bitterness?— What shadow next appears? Werner. An aged man, Lean-framed and haggard-visaged, bowed beneath The weight of years, or worldly cares that press Still heavier than the iron hand of time. His tottering form is fearful to behold! If the fierce scourge which men on earth call famine, Could incarnate itself, methinks 'twould choose Just such a shape, so worn and grim and gaunt, And wo-begone of aspect. Groping round He gathers from the burning floor of hell Some shining pebbles, which his fond conceit Transmutes to gold, and these with constant care He watches, counting and recounting them, Till suddenly a whirlwind, sweeping by, Bears with it all his fancied hoards away, Leaving him to renew his bootless task, Which ever he renews with this complaint, — "Alas! how speedily may wealth take wing." And on his front his name is written, "Avarice." Spirit. There yet is, in this shadowy land of shades, One form which I would have thee look upon. Behold it cometh! mark and scan it well. Werner. Never before in all my wanderings Through earth, or other regions, where abide Things now no more of earth, have I beheld Aught so profoundly mournful or so lone! So dark a cloud o'erhangs his haggard brow, That where he turns a dunner, murkier gloom Prevails along hell's blasting atmosphere! Surrounded by some goodly forms he moves, Forms bright as his is dark, who each in turn Woo his acceptance of the gifts they proffer. Love stretches out his dimpled band, wherein He holds his emblematic rose, and Hope, Bright Hope, that might renew again the pulse Of life within the frozen veins of Death! Beckons him to the future, — and calm Faith Kindles beneath his eye her beacon blaze; Yet, with such anguish as hell only holds, He turns him from all these, and will not take Love's proffered rose, lest 'neath its blushing leaves Should lurk the stinging thorn of sly deceit. Hope's smile to him is disappointment's signal, — And the bright beacon Faith so kindly lights To guide us o'er the treacherous sea of life, To him is but a cheat, a mockery, An ignis fatuus, kindled to mislead. And yet he seems as one who in his life Had nursed bright dreams, and cherished lofty aims, — Had dreamed of love, or wooed Ambition's smiles, Or to the sway of empires had aspired, Or, higher still, the sway of human hearts! Why gazest thou on me and not on him? Spirit. To mark if in thine aspect I might not Detect a consciousness that I thy own soul Claimed brotherhood with his! Thou too hast scoffed At human love, and hope, and faith, and truth, Nursing within thy bosom pride, and scorn, And rankling hate, I till these at length became Fiends which thou could'st not master! Thou art warned, Be wise and heed the warning. Let us now Return unto thy far off, native orb, O'er which the rosy smile of morn is breaking, Waking its teeming millions to renew Their daily rounds of toil and strife and crime. [Exeunt.

ACT IV.

Scene I. A peak of the Alps. Werner alone. Time, morning.
Werner. How gloriously beautiful is earth! In these her quiet,
unfrequented haunts, To which, except the timid chamois'
foot, Or venturous hunter's, or the eagle's wing, Naught from
beneath ascends. As yet the sun But darts his earliest rays of
golden light Upon the summits of the tallest peaks, Which
robed in clouds and capped with glittering ice, Soar proudly
up, and beam and blaze aloft, As if they would claim kindred
with the stars! And they may claim such kindred, for there is
Within, around, and over them, the same Supreme, eternal,
all-creating spirit Which glows and burns in every beaming
orb That circles in immeasurable space! Far as the eye can
trace the mountain's crest On either hand, a gorgeous, varied
mass Of glowing, cloud-formed ranges are at rest, Reflecting
back in every hue and tint, Purple and crimson, orange and
bright gold, The sunny smile with which Morn hails the
world. Beneath me all is quiet yet and calm, For the dim
shadow of the silent night Still rests upon the valley, still the
flock Sleeps undisturbed within the guarded fold, The lark
yet slumbers in her lowly nest, The dew hangs heavy upon
leaf and blade, The gray mist still o'erveils the unruffled lake,
And all is tranquil as an infant's sleep; Tranquil around me,
but not so within, For in my breast a thousand restless
thoughts Conflict in wild, chaotical confusion. Thoughts of
long bygone years, and things that were But are no more,
and thoughts that sternly strive To grapple with the mysteries I late Have looked upon; for I, since yesternight, Have
traversed the wide sea of space that rolls Between the shores
of this and other worlds; Have gazed upon and scanned
those worlds, or shades That wear the lineaments of such;
have seen The damned in their own place, and marked the
deep, Terrific retribution Error brings To such as are her vo-
taries in life. And now I feel how baseless was my hope That

Peace, the solitary boon I crave, Might spring from knowledge. Tis a fatal tree, Which ever hath borne bitter fruit, since first 'Twas set in Paradise. But I must seek The cottage of some honest mountaineer, Who may afford me nurture and repose, For I am weary, both in mind and frame. [Exit. Scene II. A chamber in the cottage of Manuel. Albert asleep. Rebecca standing by his couch. Rebecca. My boy! my beautiful, my dearest hope! The garner where my trust of future joy Is treasured. Heaven bless thee! May thy life, If it seem good to Him who gave it, be Blest to the fulness of a mother's prayer! [She stoops to kiss him, and continues. How well his sleep portrays a quiet mind, The embodied image of a sunny day, A day without a cloud, whose only voices Arise from sighing airs, and whispering leaves, And tell-tale brooks that of their banks beseech A gift, a wreath of their sweet flowers, wherewith To soothe the angry Geni of the deep! And free, glad birds that flit from bough to bough, And ring their songs of love in the clear air, Till heaven is filled with gushing melody, And the all-glowing horizon becomes A thing of life, whose breath is sweetest music! [Kisses him again, and continues. His brow to me is as a spotless page, Whereon is traced the story of my first And only love, the bright and holy dream That stole into my bosom, when beside The crystal stream that threads a neighbouring vale, I and his father watched our fathers' flocks, And he would lay aside his shepherd's pipe, And in low words, far sweeter than its music, Talk of the sun and stars and gentle moon, The earth and all its loveliness, the trees And shrubs and flowers; how these were all pervaded And quickened by the spirit of deep love; Till, by the frequent blush that tinged my cheek, The light that would break from my downcast eyes, And the quick beat of my too happy heart, Emboldened, he poured out his own pure passion, On my enchanted ear! Since then my life Has had no eras, — days, and months, and years, Have all gone by uncounted, in the full, Deep, fervent, soul-sufficing happiness, Of all I prayed for, panted for, obtained! But I must rouse him, it is time his flock Should leave the fold, and — [The boy starts and murmurs in his sleep. Down by yonder stream, Where the green willows cluster thickest, there They dwell. 'Tis scarce so far as I could cast A pebble from my sling. Seek it, and they Will minister to thee what thou mayest need. [He awakes, and recognising his mother, exclaims— Ah, mother! I have dreamed so strange a dream, So strange, and yet so palpable, that I Believed it a reality. Methought As closely followed by my bleating flock, I climbed the rugged mountain side where spring Our greenest pastures, singing as I went, I met a lonely wanderer in my way, Of brow so pale, and eye so darkly sad, That my own heart, to sadness little used, Grew heavy at the sight; and he seemed worn And very weary, not so much with toil As by some hidden, inward strife of soul, Which even then seemed raging in his breast. He stayed to question me where he might find The cottage of some honest mountaineer, Where he might crave the boons of rest and food,— And mindful of the lesson taught by thee, To give the hungry bread, the weary rest, I pointed him to where our cottage stands, Assuring him that thou and my sweet sister,— Fair as aught earthly, and as pure as fair,— Would entertain him as a welcome guest: And so we parted. Rebecca. Thou didst well to mind The lesson I so often have repeated. It is our first of duties to give aid To those who beg for succour at our hands; For we ourselves, whatever we possess, Are but the stewards of the bounteous Lord Who giveth to his creatures all good gifts. But it is time that thou shouldst seek the hills, So take thy crook and pipe and hie away. [Exeunt. Scene III. The side of a mountain. Werner descending. Enter a shepherd boy, followed by his flock, singing. I. When the Morning starts up from her couch on the deep, Where through the dim night hours, she pillows her sleep, I start from my slumbers, and hie me away Where the white torrent dashes its feathery spray,— I quaff the fresh stream as it bursts from the hill,— I pluck the fresh flowers that spring by the rill,— I watch the gray clouds as they curl round the peak That rises high over them, barren and bleak; And I think how the worldling who courts fortune's smile, In his heart, like that peak, may be lonely the while; And then my own heart sings aloud in its joy, That Heaven has made me a free shepherd boy! II. When the horn of the hunter resounds from on high, Where the tall giant ice-cliffs ire piled to the sky, Where, shunning the verdure of valleys and dells, The brave eagle builds, and the shy chamois dwells,— I list to its gay tones, as by me they float, And I echo them merrily back, note for note; With the wild bird a song full as gladsome I sing, I crown me with flowers, and sit a crowned king,— My flock are my subjects, my dog my vizier, And my sceptre—a mild one—the crook that I bear; No wants to perplex me, no cares to annoy, I live an unenvying, free shepherdboy! Werner (meets and addresses him). Thou'rt merry, lad. Albert. Ay, I have cause to be so. (Aside.) It is the wanderer of my last night's dream, The same pale brow, and darkly mournful eye, And weary gait, and melancholy voice,— If he seeks friendly guidance, food, or shelter, He shall not want them long. Werner. So thou hast cause For merriment,— then thou perchance hast wealth, Broad, fruitful lands, and tenements, and all Which wealth confers. Albert. Nay, I have none of these, And yet have more than all which thou hast named. I have a father, whose unsullied name No tongue has ever spoken with reproach, A mother, whose idea is with me A holy thing, and a dear sister, who Is fair as pure, and pure as is the snow Upon the summit of the tallest peak Of these my native mountains. I have health, And strength, and food, and raiment, and employ, And should I not then have a joyous heart? Werner. Yea, verily thou shouldst. Albert. And there is yet, Among the blessings Heaven has given to me, One which I have not named to thee; it is An humble home, whose hospitable door Was never closed against the wayfarer,— If thou hast need of aught which it affords, Seek it, my mother and my sister will Delight to minister unto thy wants. There where the wide-armed willows cluster thickest Upon the green banks of yon crystal stream, Our cottage stands. The path to it is short And easily traversed,—so, now, farewell. Werner. Stay yet a moment. That which thou hast proffered, Is what I sought. Thou hast a noble heart, One fit to fill the bosom of a king,— I fain would give thee guerdon,—here is gold. Albert. Keep it for those who covet it. If ever Thou meet'st with one, bowed down by suffering, Who calls on thee for pity and relief, Then if thou heed'st his prayer for my sake, I shall be well repaid. Again, farewell. {Exeunt. Scene IV. After a lapse of time. A rustic arbour near the cottage of Manuel. Enter Rose and Werner. Rose. Nay, let my silent blushes plead with thee That thou wilt be as silent. Werner. Rather let My ardent love, which will not be repressed, Plead with thee for acceptance of my suit; For I do love thee with such passionate love, That life itself, if weighed against that love, Were scarce a feather in the scale. Rose. Alas! I'm but a simple shepherd's simple child, Unused to courtly speeches, and they say That in the world thy name and rank are high, And that when such as thou do proffer love And faith to lowly maidens, 'tis a jest,— And that when they have won our honest love, They cast it from them with unpitying hands, As idly as they would a withered flower. Werner. Nay, maiden, let me tell thee of the past, Let me lay bare my heart beneath thy gaze, And thou wilt pity if thou canst not love. I loved in youth with love as fond and deep As ever made the heart of man its slave, But, ere my hopes could ripen to fruition, Death came and made my worshipped one his prize; And though my peace departed when she died, Yet I was proud, and would not bond to sorrow, But with calm brow and eye, and smiling lip, I mingled with the giddy thoughtless world, Seeking from out its varied realms to wring Some recompense for that which I had lost. Wealth, fame, and power, I sought for and obtained, Yet found them only gilded mockeries. The paths of hidden knowledge I essayed, And trod their mazy windings till they led My footsteps—whither I may not disclose,— But all availed me nothing, still my heart Ached with the dreary void lost love had made, Ached ever till that void was filled by thee! Since first fate led me to your kindly door, Three times the moon with full-orbed light hath shone, Thrice thirty times, with song of merry birds And breath of fragrance, Morn has blest the earth And all its dwellers with her radiant presence; Thrice thirty times, with star-bound brow, dim Night Hath kept her tearful watch above the earth; And every time the full-orb'd moon hath shone, And every time the merry Morn hath smiled, And every time dim Night with star-bound brow Above the earth hath kept her tearful watch, My heart has added to its store of love, Its pure, deep, fervent, passionate love for thee! By all my hopes of heaven, my words are true. Dost thou not pity now? Rose. Ay, more! My heart, And its full treasury of maiden love, Never before surrendered to another, I pledge to thee, as thine, for evermore! [Exeunt. An Aerial Chorus. Seek the dell and seek the bower, Pluck the bud and pluck the flower, Search for buds of sweetest breath, Search for flowers of brightest hue; Fit to weave the bridal wreath, Of a maid so fair and true. She has bowed the haughty heart, Won the stubborn will from guile, With no aid of other art Than the sweet spell of her smile! Seek the dell and seek the bower, Pluck the bud and pluck the flower, Search for buds of sweetest breath, Search for flowers of brightest hue; Fit to weave the bridal wreath, Of a maid so fair and true! [Exeunt.

Note to the Misanthrope

"Then seek we, for the maiden's pillow, Far beyond the Atlantic's billow, Love's apple,—and when we have found it, Draw the magic circles round it."

Considering the Mandrake, many fabulous notions were entertained by the ancients; and they never attempted to extract it from the earth, without the previous performance of such ceremonies as they considered efficacious in preventing the numerous accidents, dangers, and diseases, to which they believed the person exposed who was daring enough to undertake its extraction. The usual manner of obtaining it was this:—When found, three times a circle was drawn around it with the point of a naked sword, and a dog was then attached to it and beaten, until by his struggles it was disengaged from the earth.

It was supposed to be useful in producing dreams, philters, charms &c.; and also to possess the faculties of exciting love, and increasing population.

The Emperor Adrian, in a letter to Calexines, writes that he is drinking the juice of the Mandrake to render him amorous: hence it was called Love-apple.

It grows in Italy, Spain, and the Levant.

MISCELLANEOUS POEMS

TO ISABEL

A Beautiful Little Girl. Fair as some sea-child, in her coral bower, Decked with the rare, rich treasures of the deep; Mild as the spirit of the dream whose power Bears back the infant's soul to heaven, in sleep Brightens the hues of summer's first-born flower Pure as the tears repentant mourners weep O'er deeds to which the siren, Sin, beguiled, — Art thou, sweet, smiling, bright-eyed cherub child. Thy presence is a spell of holiness, From which unhallowed thoughts shrink blushing back, — Thy smile is a warm light that shines to bless, As beams the beacon o'er the wanderer's track, — Thy voice is music, at whose sounds Distress Unbinds her writhing victim from the rack Of misery, and charmed by what she hears, Forgets her woes, and smiles upon her tears. And when I look upon thee, bearing now The promise of such loveliness, I ask If time will blight, that promise; if thy brow, So sunny now, will learn to wear the mask Of hollow smiles, or cold deceit, whilst thou Art learning in thy soul the bitter task Time teaches to all bosoms, when the glow Of hope is o'er — but this I may not know. My path will not be near to thine through life, — Kind ones will guard and fondly shelter thee; Me bitterness awaits, and care and strife, And all that sorrow has of agony; My future, as my past was, will be rife With heartaches, and the pangs that "pass not by;" Each hour shall give thee some new pleasure; years, Long years can bring me only toil 'and tears. 'Tis meet that it should be so, — I have made A wreck of my own happiness, and cast Across my heart, in youth, the dull, deep shade That wrinkled age flings over all at last But let it go, — I have too long delayed The remedy, and what is past is past; — And could I live those vanished moments o'er, My heart would wander as it strayed before. I know not how it is,—my heart is stern, And little giv'n to thoughts of tenderness; Yet looking on thy young brow it will yearn, And in my bosom's innermost recess, Thoughts that have slumbered long awake and burn With a wild strength which nothing can repress! Be still, worn heart, be still; does not the cold And heavy clay—clod mingle with her mould? Yes, 'tis that in thy soft check's tender bloom, Thy black eyes' brightness, in each graceful move, I trace the lineaments of one to whom My soul was wedded in an early love,— 'Twas in my boyhood; but the insatiate tomb Claimed her fair form, and for the realms above Her spirit fled the earth; oh! how I wept That mine should in its bondage still be kept. I mind the hour I stood beside the clay I had so loved in life—it still was fair, Surpassing fair, in death; and as she lay With the thick tresses of her long dark hair Gathered above the brow whence feeling's ray Had fled, because death's shadow darkened there, Her more than earthly beauty made her seem The incarnation of some pure bright dream. I stood and gazed: the pale grave sheet was wound About the form from which life's spark was fled, For ever fled,—wet eyes were weeping round, And voices full of sorrow mourned the dead; I could not weep; a sadness more profound Than that from which those heart-drops, tears, are shed, Was in my soul,—for then the icy spell Of desolation freezing o'er me fell. And from that hour I have been alone, Alone when crowds were round me. May thy fate Be coloured with a brighter hue, and strown With flowers where mine is thorns;—where mine is hate, And strife, and bitter discord, may thine own Be love, and hope, and peace—for these create The sunshine of existence; may their light Beam ever round thee, warm, and glad, and bright.

THE LOCK OF HAIR.

It is in sooth a lovely tress, Still curled in many a ring, As glossy as the plumes that dress The raven's jetty wing. And the broad and soul-illumined brow, Above whose arch it grew, Was like the stainless mountain snow, In its purity of hue. I mind the time 'twas given to me, The night, the hour, the spot; And the eye that pleaded silently, "Forget the giver not." Oh! myriads of stars, on high, Were smiling sweetly fair, But none was lovely as the eye That shone beside me there! Above our heads an ancient oak Its strong, wide arms held out, And from its roots a fountain broke, With a tiny laughing shout; And the fairy people of the wild Were bending to their rest, As trustingly as sleeps the child Upon its mother's breast. Soft, silvery cloudlets, pure and white, Along the sky were hung, As if the spirits of the night Their mantles there had flung; And then the night-breeze pensively Sighed from its unseen throne, And far o'er field, and flower, and tree, A hallowed light came down. But in our breasts was springing up A something lovelier far, Than field, or tree, or flow'ret's cup, Or sun, or moon, or star! We heeded not the fountain near, Its song of gladness singing, For in our hearts a fount more dear, And pure, and sweet, was springing. And she was one whom fortune's smile Had gladdened from her birth, Yet her high spirit knew no guile, No blot nor stain of earth; And I was but a friendless boy, And yet her heart was mine; I knew it, and the thought was joy, A joy all, all divine! From out a braided mass she took This single lock of jet, And gave it with that pleading look Which, said, "Do not forget." Forget! as soon the waves that roll The ocean's caves above, May tell their secrets, as the soul Forget its earliest love. It has been with me now for years, Long years of care and strife, And shall be with me till time wears Away my web of life. And when death's keen, resistless dart, Shall bid its sorrows cease, This tress shall rest upon my heart, Its talisman of peace.

"'Twas little she thought that I stood breathless by her side listening to the song she sang as she sat by the sea's edge, pondering so deeply, upon me too perhaps, that the white foam glimmered on her brow unheeded." Onagh, The Pale Child of the Brehon King. She stood beside the wide wild sea, The winds howled hoarse and high, And dark clouds, drifting drearily, Swept o'er the starless sky. Her breast was white as mountain snow, Her locks hung loose and free, The foam that glimmered on her brow, Was scarce so pale as she. She sang a mournful song of love, Of trusting love betrayed; Ah, why did he who won her, prove So faithless to the maid? "Why pines my heart so wearily, Why heaves my aching breast, And why is sleep so far from me, When others are at rest? "Thou, truant wanderer o'er the deep, The cause of all my cares; For thee at night I wake and weep, When none may mark my tears. "I seek the festive hall no more, Its mirth no more I crave; My heart is lonely as the shore, And restless as the wave. "My soul has struggled to forget Its sleepless, fatal flame; I know thy vows were false, and yet My love is still the same. "Still o'er the dream I nursed too well, My bursting heart will yearn; For ever with me must it dwell, — Oh, wanderer, return!" A white sail fluttered in the wind, A light bark skimmed the sea, — It came like hope across the mind, As swift and silently. The shell-strewn beach that edged the main, A manly footstep pressed; The wanderer had returned again, — The maiden's heart was blessed!

THE DESERTED.

"Come, sit thee by my side once more, 'Tis long since thus we' met; And though our dream of love is o'er, Its sweetness lingers yet. Its transient day has long been past, Its flame has ceased to burn, — But Memory holds its spirit fast, Safe in her sacred urn. "I will not chide thy wanderings, Nor ask why thou couldst flee A heart whose deep affection's springs Poured forth such love for thee! We may not curb the restless mind, Nor teach the wayward heart To love against its will, nor bind It with the chains of art. "I would but tell thee how, in tears And bitterness, my soul Has yearned with dreams, through long, long, years, Which it could not control. And how the thought that clingeth to, And twineth round the past, For ever in my heart shall glow, And be save one my last. "They say thou hast another's love, — Well, cherish it, but thou Its lack of strength and depth wilt prove, Should sorrow cloud thy brow. Though she may own a statelier form, A fairer cheek than mine, Her heart cannot so well and warm, Respond each throb of thine." Her words were gentle, but their tone Was sad as sorrow's sigh, — A tear-drop trembled in his own As he sought her downcast eye. A chord was struck within his breast That long untouched had lain, Old memories started from their rest, — The maid was loved again. Stanzas. On! there are hours of sadness, when the soul, Torn from its every stay, and crushed beneath Its many griefs, and spurning faith's control, Pants with an earnest longing for the death Which would for ever close its dark career, With the pale shroud and the remorseless bier; When the harsh, sterile nothingness of life, First breaks upon the hope-deluded breast, And the heart sickens with the bootless strife That wrings its chords, and longs to be at rest; Ev'n if the blow that frees it from distress, Should strike it into utter nothingness. Ah, nothingness! The thought at times will come, The mind will wrestle with the mystery That clouds its being! from its clay-made home, Its dwelling of a moment, it will flee Into the far depths of the vast UNKNOWN, In its vain searchings for th' eternal throne Of that Omnipotence which gave it birth, And, giving it a nature which might suit A seraph, bound its destiny to earth! And a few years, in which to eat the fruit Of life's strange tree, so bitter at its core, Then death, the quiet grave, sleep, and — what more? Whence came we? whither go we? All is still And voiceless in the past! A veil is drawn Across the future! by life's mystic rill We sit and ponder, watching for the dawn Of some yet unconceived, far-reaching thought, By which our nature's secret shall be taught! Why sorrow is our element — why sin Is native in us — by what curse we bear An ever aching, crushing void within Our secret souls! and why the little share Of happiness that mingles with our fate, Is of such fleeting, transitory date 1 Our loves! our hopes! what are they? fruits which turn To ashes on our lips! illusive lights That cast a moment's brightness while they burn, Then die, and leave a darkness which affrights Our spirits with its thrice redoubled gloom, Making the sky a pall — the earth a tomb! And yet these are the all of life for which 'Tis worth the wearing of its chain to know, Wealth, fame, and power are but toys! the rich, The high and mighty, with the base and low, Alike before the reaper Death must fall, — So be it! in the grave is rest for all. Stanzas. When the leaf is on the tree, And the bird is in the bower, And the butterfly and bee, Bear its treasures from the flower; When the fields put on the sheen, That to young-eyed Spring belongs; When the groves and forests green, Echo with a thousand songs; When wild Beauty wanders forth, Giving, with no stinted care, All her loveliness to earth, All her sweetness to the air: Then the heart, with gladness stirred, Mindful of its griefs no more, Mounts and carols, like a bird When the pearly shower is o'er! But the summer's sunny hours, As we count them, pass away; And its fairest fruits and flowers, Are but food for stern decay. Then with wailings, deep and loud, Like the sea's in its unrest, Winter spreads his icy shroud, O'er the bare earth's frozen breast. Thus the spirit's early gladness, Sorrow chills or time removes; And the soul, in tears and sadness, Mourns its perished joys and loves. Hope will lose its trusting boldness, One by one its beams depart, And Despair, with icy, coldness, Winds its mantle round the heart.

AFTER WITNESSING A DEATH-SCENE.

Press close your lips, And bow your heads to earth, for Death is here! Mark ye not how across that eye so clear, Steals his eclipse? A moment more, And the quick throbbings of her heart shall cease, Her pain-wrung spirit will obtain release,

And all be o'er! Hush! Seal ye up Your gushing tears, for Mercy's hand hath shaken Her earth-bonds off, and from her lip hath taken Grief's bitter cup. Ye know the dead Are they who rest secure from care and strife, — That they who walk the thorny way of life, Have tears to shed. Ye know her pray'r, Was for the quiet of the tomb's deep rest, — Love's sepulchre lay cold within her breast, Could peace dwell there? A tale soon told, Is of her life the story; she had loved, And he who won her heart to love, had proved Heartless and cold. Lay her to rest, Where shines and falls the summer's sun and dew; For these should shine and fall where lies so true And fond a breast! A full release From every pang is given to the dead, — So on the stone ye place above her head, Write only "Peace."* When Spring comes back, With music on her lips, — joy in her eye, — Her sunny banner streaming through the sky, — Flow'rs in her track — Then come ye here, And musing from the busy world apart, Drop on the turf that wraps her mouldering heart, Sweet Pity's tear.

* The most touchingly beautiful epitaph I have ever read, was written in that one word, "Peace." It seemed like the last sigh of a departing spirit, over the clay which it was about to abandon for ever.

LOVE AND FANCY.

"Whenever, amid bow'rs of myrtle, Love, summer-tressed and vernal-eyed, At morn or eve is seen to wander, A dark-haired girl is at his side." De La Hogue. One morn, just as day in the far east was breaking, Young Love, who all night had been roving about, A charming siesta was quietly taking, His strength, by his rambles, completely worn out. Round his brow a wreath, woven of every flower That springs from the hillside, or valley, was bound; In his hand was a rose he had stol'n from some bower, While his bow and his quiver lay near on the ground. Wild Fancy just came from her kingdom of dreams, The breath of the opening day to enjoy, And to catch the warm kiss of its first golden beams On her cheek, caught a glimpse of the slumbering boy! With a light, noiseless step she drew near to the sleeper, And gazed till her snowy-breast heaved a soft sigh; Then she bade sleep's dull god bring a sounder and deeper And heavier trance for Love's beautiful eye. Then back to her shadowy kingdom she flow, And called up the bright mystic forms she has there; And filling an urn from a fountain of dew, She bade them all straight to Love's couch-side repair. They came, and stood round, as her hand, o'er his pillow, From a chalice of pearl, poured its magical stream: While his red rosy lips, that now sighed like a billow At play with the breeze, told how sweet was his dream. He dreamed that he sat on a shining throne, wrought Of the purest of gold that the earth could supply, While a trio of beautiful maids, who each brought A gift for his shrine, in succession past by. First Fame, with the step and the glance of a queen, Came up, and before him bent down her proud knee, And held up a garland, whereon played the sheen Of the beams which insure immortality! Next Wealth, the stern mistress of men, for whose smile They toil like the galley slave,—brought in her hand The fair gems of many an ocean isle, And the diamonds of many a far off land. And Beauty came too, with her blue, laughing eye, Her fair flowing locks, and her soft rosy cheek, And red lips, whose sweet smile told silently The tale which they seemed ashamed to speak. 'Neath the shade of a palm branch a fourth one stood by, With locks like in hue to the tresses of Night, With a pale, pensive brow, and a dark dreamy eye, Where the soul of sweet softness lay gleaming in light! It was Fancy: Love gazed, and his eager eye shone With a lustre of feeling, deep, fervent, and sweet; And he thought it were better to give up his throne For a place, on his knees, at the coy maiden's feet. And from that bright hour, through calm and through storm, Through the sunlight of summer, and winter's dark reign, These twain have been bound by ties, tender and warm, Which ne'er through all time shall be severed again. And ever where Love weaves his fond witchery, Will

Fancy the aid of her brightness bestow, And give the loved object, whatever it be, A purer, a dearer, a heavenlier glow!

LINES WRITTEN IN A YOUNG LADY'S ALBUM

'Tis not in youth, when life is new, when but to live is sweet, When Pleasure strews her starlike flow'rs beneath our careless feet, When Hope, that has not been deferred, first waves its golden wings, And crowds the distant future with a thousand lovely things; — When if a transient grief o'ershades the spirit for a while, The momentary tear that falls is followed by a smile; Or if a pensive mood, at times, across the bosom steals, It scarcely sighs, so gentle is the pensiveness it feels It is not then the, restless soul will seek for one with whom To share whatever lot it bears, its gladness or its gloom, — Some trusting, tried, and gentle heart, some true and faithful breast, Whereon its pinions it may fold, and claim a place of rest. But oh! when comes the icy chill that freezes o'er the heart, When, one by one, the joys we shared, the hopes we held, depart; When friends, like autumn's withered leaves, have fallen by our side, And life, so pleasant once, becomes a desert wild and wide; — As for her olive branch the dove swept o'er the sullen wave, That rolled above the olden world — its death-robe and its grave! — So will the spirit search the earth for some kind, gentle one, With it to share her destiny, and make it all her own!

TO A LADY.

Suggested By Hearing Her Voice During Services At Church.
At night, in visions, when my soul drew near The shadowy
confines of the spirit land, Wild, wondrous notes of song
have met my ear, Wrung from their harps by many a seraph's
hand; And forms of light, too, more divinely fair Than Mercy's messenger to hearts that mourn, On wings that made
sweet music in the air, Have round me, in those hours of
bliss, been borne, And, filled with joy unutterable, I Have
deemed myself a born child of the sky. And often, too, at
sunset's magic hour, When musing by some solitary stream,
While thought awoke in its resistless pow'r, And restless
Fancy wove her brightest dream: Mysterious tongues, that
were not of the earth, Have whispered words which I may
not repeat, — But Thought or Fancy ne'er have given birth To
form and voice like thine, — so fair and sweet! Nor have I
found them when my spirit's flight Had borne me to the far
shores of delight. Above the murmurs of an hundred lips,
They rose, those silvery tones of praise and pray'r, Soft as the
light breeze, when Aurora trips The earth, and, lighting up
the darkened air, Carols her greetings to the waking flow'rs!
They fell upon my heart like summer rain Upon the thirsting
fields, — and earlier hours, When I too breathed th' adoring
pray'r and strain, Came back once more; the present was beguiled Of half its gloom, and my worn spirit smiled. Pray,
lady, that the sad, soul-searing blight, Which comes upon us
when we tread the ways Of sin, may not be suffered to alight
On thy pure spirit in its youthful days; Or like the fruitage of
the Dead Sea shore, Tho' outward bloom and freshness thou
may'st be, Stern bitterness and death will gnaw thy core, And
thou wilt be a heart-scathed thing like me, Bearing the weight
of many years, ere thou Hast lost youth's rosy cheek and line-
less brow.

IMPROMPTU, On The Reception Of A Letter. I would love to
have thee near me, But when I think how drear Is each hope
that used to cheer me, I cease to wish thee here. I know that
thou, wouldst not shrink from The storms that burst on me,

But the bitter chalice I drink from, I will not pass to thee. I would share the world with thee, were it With all its pleasures mine, But the sorrows which I inherit, I never will make thine!

THE OLD MAN AND THE BOY.

"Glenara, Glenara, now read me my dream." Campbell. Father, I have dreamed a dream, When the rosy morning hour Poured its light on field and stream, Kindling nature with its pow'r; — O'er the meadow's dewy breast, I had chased a butterfly, Tempted by its gaudy vest, Still my vain pursuit to ply, — Till my limbs were weary grown, With the distance I had strayed, Then to rest I laid me down, Where a beech tree cast its shade, Soon a heaviness came o'er me, And a deep sleep sealed my eyes; And a vision past before me, Full of changing phantasies. First I stood beside a bower, Green as summer bow'r could be; Vine and fruit, and leaf and flower, Mixed to weave its canopy. And within reclined a form, As embodied moonlight fair, With a soft cheek, fresh and warm, Deep blue eye and sunny hair. By her side a goblet stood, Such as bacchanalians brim; High the rich grape's crimson blood, Sparkled o'er its gilded rim. As I gazed, she bowed her head, With a gay and graceful move, And in words of music said, "Drink, and learn the lore of love!" Next I stood beside a mountain, Of majestic form and height; Cliff and crag, and glen and fountain, Mingled to make up its might. On its lofty brow were growing Flowers never chilled by gloom, For the sky above them glowing, Dyed them with a deathless bloom. And I saw the crystal dome, Wondrous in its majesty, Where earth's great ones find a home, When their spirits are set free. By its portals, I espied One who kept the courts within; High he waved a wreath and cried, "Come up hither, — strive and win!" Then my vision changed again: In a fairy-coloured shell, O'er the wide sea's pathless plain, I was speeding, fast and well. Suddenly, beneath its prow, Parted were the azure waves, And I saw where, far below, Yawn the vast deep's secret caves. Where the Syren sings her song, To old Ocean's sons and daughters; And the mermaids dance along, To the music of the waters. Where the coral forest o'er, Storm or tempest ne'er is driven And the gems that strew its floor, Sparkle like the stars in heaven. Treasures, such as never eye Of the earth has looked upon, Gold and pearls of many a dye, There in rich profusion shone. And a voice came to my ear, Saying, in a stern, cold tone, Such as chills the heart with fear, "Seize and make the prize thine own." Then across a clouded wild, Lone and drear and desolate, Where no cheerful cottage smiled, I pursued the steps of fate. Ever bearing in my breast, Thoughts almost to madness wrought; Ever, ever seeking rest, Never finding what I Sought — Till I gave my wanderings o'er, By a black and icy stream, — Deep I plunged and knew no more: — Father, read me now my dream. The old man bowed his head, And pressed his thin hand to his withered brow, As if he struggled with some rising thought Which should have kept its place in memory's urn Till he had cast the shadow from his soul, Which for a while had bound it in a spell Born of the bygone years, — then thus he spoke: Now listen, boy, and I will show to thee The import of thy vision, — I will tell Thee what its scenes and shapes of mystery Foreshadow of the future, — for full well I know the wizard lore, whose witchery Binds e'en the time to come in its wild spell! And from approaching years a knowledge wrings Of what they bear upon their viewless wings. Along life's weary way of pain and care, From earliest infancy to eldest age, Forms, viewless as the soft-breathed summer air, Attend man's footsteps in his pilgrimage; And if his destiny be dark or fair, If Pleasure gilds, or Sorrow blots the page Whereon is traced his history, still his ear Will ever catch their warning voices near. And they — those guardian ones, who, while thy sleep Hung o'er thee like a curtain, came around And fanned thee till thy slumber grew more deep, — Flung o'er thy rest, so perfect and profound, A dream whose mem'ry thou shouldst ever keep Bound to thy spirit, for altho' it wound, Thy young heart now, perchance,

in after years, 'Twill save thee much of toil, and many tears. It
was a dream of life: of boyhood's strong And soul-consuming
yearnings after love! His eager search to find, amid the
throng, Some heart to give him thought for thought—to
move And mingle with his own, as twines the song From
Beauty's lyre and lips! to know and prove The dearest joy to
care-cursed mortals given, The one with least of earth, and
most of heaven Of manhood's ceaseless strivings after
fame,— The veriest phantom of all phantasies— For which
he wields the sword, or lights the flame Whose red glare
mocks a nation's agonies,— Or by his star-outwatching taper,
plies His pen or pencil, to gain—what? a name, A passing
sound—an echo—a mere breath, Which he, vain fool, dreams
mightier than death! And of a later period, when the soul
Forsakes its high resolves and wild desires, When stern Ambition can no more control, And Love has shrouded o'er its
smothered fires; When Expectation ceases to console, And
Hope, the last kind comforter, expires; And Avarice, monster
of the gilded vest, Creeps in and occupies the vacant breast.
And then the last sad scene: The sick heart, sore And fainting
from its wounds—the palsied limb— The brow whose death-
sweat peeps from every pore— The eye with its long, weary
watch grown dim— The withered, wan cheek, that shall
bloom no more— The last dregs dripping slowly from the
brim Of life's drained cup,—behind all gloom, before A deep,
dark gulf—we plunge, and all is o'er!

ACLE AT THE GRAVE OF NERO.

It is a circumstance connected with the history of Nero, that every
spring and summer, for many years after his death, fresh and beautiful flowers were nightly scattered upon his grave by some unknown hand.

Tradition relates that it was done by a young maiden of Corinth,
named Acle, whom Nero had brought to Rome from her native city,

whither he had gone in the disguise of an artist, to contend in the Nemean, Isthinian, and Floral games, celebrated there; and whence he returned conqueror in the Palaestra, the chariot race, and the song; bearing with him, like Jason of old, a second Medea, divine in form and feature as the first, and who like her had left father, friends, and country, to follow a stranger.

Even the worse than savage barbarity of this sanguinary tyrant, had not cut him off from all human affection; and those flowers were doubtless the tribute of that young girl's holy and enduring love!

> Whose name is on yon lettered stone? whose ashes rest beneath? That thus you come with flowers to deck the mournful home of death; And thou — why darkens so thy brow with grief's untimely gloom? Thou art fitter for a bride than for a watcher by the tomb! "It is the name of one whose deeds made men grow pale with fear, And Nero's, stranger, is the dust that lies sepulchred here; That name may be a word of harsh and boding sound to thee, But oh! it has a more than mortal melody for me! "And I, — my heart has grown to age in girlhood's fleeting years, And has one only task — to bathe its buried love in tears; The all of life that yet remains to me is but its breath; Then tell me, is it meet that I should seek the bridal wreath?" But maiden, he of whom you speak was of a savage mood, That took its joy alone in scenes, of carnage, tears and blood; His dark, wild spirit bore the stain of crime's most loathsome hue, And love is for the high of soul — the gentle and the true. "The voice that taught an abject world to tremble at its words, To me was mild and musical, and mellow as a bird's — A bird's — that couched among the green, broad branches of the date, Tells, in its silvery songs, its gushing gladness to its mate. "I saw him first beside the sea; near to ray father's home, When like an ocean deity he bounded from the foam; Ev'n then a glory seemed to breathe around him as he trod, And my haughty soul was bowed, as in the presence of a God. I knew not, till my heart was his, the darkness of his own, Nor dreamed that he who knelt to me was master of a throne! And when the fearful knowledge

came, its coming was in vain, — I had forsaken all for him,
and would do so again." Is love the offspring of the will? or is
it, like a flower, So frail that it may fade and be forgotten in
an hour? No, no! it springs unbidden where the heart's deep
fountains play, And cherished by their hallowed dew, it cannot pass away!

THE VENETIAN GIRL'S EVENING SONG.

Unmoor the skiff, — unmoor the skiff, — The night wind's sigh
is on the air, And o'er the highest Alpine cliff, The pale moon
rises, broad and clear. The murmuring waves are tranquil
now, And on their breast each twinkling star With which
Night gems her dusky brow, Flings its mild radiance from
afar. Put off upon the deep blue sea, And leave the banquet
and the ball; For solitude, when shared with thee, Is dearer
than the carnival. And in my heart are thoughts of love, Such
thoughts as lips should only breathe, When the bright stars
keep watch above, And the calm waters sleep beneath! The
tale I have for thee, perchance, May to thine eye anew impart
The long-lost gladness of its glance, And soothe the sorrows
of thy heart; Come, I will sing for thee again, The songs
which once our mothers sung, Ere tyranny its galling chain
On them, and those they loved, had hung. Thou'rt sad; thou
say'st that in the halls Which echoed once our father's tread,
The stranger's idle footstep falls, With sound that might
awake the dead! The mighty dead! whose dust around An
atmosphere of reverence sheds; If aught of earthly voice or
sound, Might reach them in their marble beds. That she to
whom the deep gave birth, — Fair Venice! to whose queenly
stores The wealth and beauty of the earth Were wafted from
an hundred shores! Now on her wave-girt site, forlorn, Sits
shrouded in affliction's night, — The object of the tyrant's
scorn, Sad monument of fallen might. Well, tho' in her de-
serted halls The fire on Freedom's shrine is dead, Tho' o'er

her darkened, crumbling walls, Stern Desolation's pall is spread; Is not the second better part, To that which rends the despot's chain, To wear it with a dauntless heart, To feel yet shrink not from its pain? Then let the creeping ivy twine Its wreaths about each ruined arch, Till Time shall crush them in the brine, Beneath its all-triumphant march! Then let the swelling waters close Above the sea-child's sinking frame, And hide for ever from her foes, Each trace and vestige of her shame. Shall we at last less calmly sleep, When in the narrow death-house pent, Because the bosom of the deep Shall be our only monument? No! by the waste of waters bid, Our tombs as well shall keep their trust, As tho' a marble pyramid Were piled above our mangled dust!

Written in the National Gallery, at the city of Washington, on looking at a Mummy, supposed to have belonged to a race extinct before the occupation of the Western Continent by the people in whose possession the Europeans found it.

Sole and mysterious relic of a race That long has ceased to be, whose very name, Time, ever bearing on with steady pace, Has swept away from earth, leaving thy frame, Darkened by thirty centuries, to claim, Among the records of the things that were, Its place, — Tradition has forgot thee — Fame, If ever fame was thine, has ceased to bear Her record of thee, — say, what dost thou here? Three thousand years ago a mother's arms Were wrapped about that dark and ghastly form, And all the loveliness of childhood's charms Glowed on that cheek, with life then flushed and warm; Say, what preserved thee from the hungry worm That haunts with gnawing tooth the gloomy bed Spread for the lifeless? Tell what could disarm Decay of half its power, and while it fed On empires — races — make it spare the dead! How strange to contemplate the wondrous story, When those deep sunken eyes first saw the light, Lost Babylon was in her midday glory, — Upon her pride and power had fall'n no blight; And Tyre, the ancient mariner's delight, Whose merchantmen were princes, and whose name Was theme of praise to all, has left her site To utter barren nakedness and shame, — Yet thou, amid all change, art still the same. And she who, by the "yellow Tiber's" side, Sits wrapped in her dark veil of widowhood, With scarce a glimmer of her ancient pride, To cheer the gloom of that deep solitude Which o'er the seat of vanquished pow'r doth brood, Since thou wast born has seen her glories rise, Burn, and expire! quenched by the streams of blood Which her slaves drew from her own veins, the price Of usurpation, proud Ambition's sacrifice! And darker in her fate, and sadder still, The sacred city of the minstrel king, That proudly sat on Zion's holy hill, The wonder of the world! Destruction's wing Hath from her swept each fair and goodly thing; Her palaces and temples! where are they? Her walls and marble tow'rs lie mouldering, Her glory to the spoiler's hand a prey, — And yet time spares a portion of thy clay! And thou art here amid a stranger race, To whom these shores four centuries ago, Tho' now proud Freedom's boasted dwelling-place, Were all unknown; the wide streams that now flow Where Cultivation's hand has steered her plough, Had then but seen the forest huntsman guide His light canoe across the waves which now Reflect the snowy sails that waft in pride The stately ship along their rippling tide. Thou art the silent messenger of ages, Sent back to tread with Time his constant way, To shame the wisdom of conceited sages, Whose lore is but a thing of yesterday; What would their best, their brightest visions weigh Beside the fearful truths thou couldst reveal? The secrets of eternity now lay Unveiled before thee, and for we or weal, Thy doom is fixed beyond ev'n heaven's repeal. I will not ask thee of the mysteries That lie beyond Death's shadowy vale; but thou Mayst tell us of the fate the Destinies Wove for thine earthly sojourn. Was thy brow Graced with the poet's, hero's garland? How Dealt Fortune with thee? Did she curse or bless Thee with her frown or smile? Speak! thou art now Among the living, — they around thee press. Still silent? Then thy lot we can but guess. Perhaps thou wast a monarch, and hast worn The sceptre of some real El Dorado! Perhaps a warrior, and those arms have borne The foremost shield, and dealt the deadliest blow That drew the life-blood of a warring foe! Perhaps thou wor'st the courtier's gilded thrall, — Some glittering court's gay, proud papilio! Perchance a clown, the jester of some hall, The slave of one man, and the fool of all! Oh life! and pride! and honour! come and see To what a depth your visions tumble down! Behold your wearer, — who shall say if he Were monarch, warrior, parasite, or clown! And ye, who talk of glory and renown, And call them bright and deathless! and who break Each dearer tie to grasp fame's gilded crown, Come, hear instruction from this shadow speak, And learn how valueless the prize ye seek! See where ambition's loftiest flight doth tend, Behold the doom perhaps of blood-bought fame, And know that all which earth can give must end, In dust and ashes, and an empty name! Ye passions! which defy our pow'r to tame Or curb your headlong tides, behold your home! Love! see the breast where thou didst light thy flame! Immortal spirit! see thy shattered dome! When shall its hour of renovation come? Shall life possess, and beauty deck again That withered form, and foul and dusky cheek? Will Death resign his dull and frozen reign, And the immortal soul return to seek Her long-deserted dwelling, and to break The bondage which has held in icy chains All that was mortal of thee? will she make Her home in thee, and shall these poor remains Share with her heaven's pleasures or hell's pains? Wonder of wonders! who could look on thee And afterward survey with curious eye The mouldering shrines where dupes have bent the knee, Where superstition, by hypocrisy Nurtured and fed with tales of mystery, Has oft with timid footstep trembling trod, — All these are worse than nothing; come and see Where once a deathless soul held its abode, — The wrecked and ruined palace of a God! Farewell! Not idly has this hour been spent. Thy silent teachings I may not forget, — More deeply, strangely, truly eloquent, Than all the babbled words which ever yet Have fall'n from living lips, — they shall be set With the bright gems which Wisdom loves to keep; And when my spirit against fate would fret, My eyes shall turn to thee and cease to weep, Till I too sleep death's deep and dreamless sleep!

TO ISABEL.

Come near me with thy lips, and, breathe o'er mine Their
breath, for I consume with love's desire, — Thine ivory arms
about me clasp and twine, And beam upon mine eye thine
eye's soft fire; Clasp me yet closer, till my heart feels thine
Thrill, as the chords of Memnon's mystic lyre Thrilled at the
sun's uprising! thou who art The lone, the worshipped idol of
my heart! There! balmier than the south wind, when it brings
The scent of aromatic shrub and tree, And tropic flower on ifs
glowing wings, Thine odorous breath is wafted over me;
How to thy dewy lips mine own lip clings, And my whole
being is absorbed in thee; And in my breast thine eyes have
lit a fire That never, never, never shall expire! Eternal — is it
not eternal — this Our passionate love? what pow'r shall part
us twain? Not even Death! Life could bestow no bliss Like
death with thee, and I would rend its chain If thou shouldst
perish, for my heaven is To gaze upon thee! I could bear all
pain Unsighing, so not parted from thy side, My beautiful!
my spirit's chosen bride! They try to woo me from thy fond
embrace, To lure me from the light of those dear eyes; They
tell me that in fortune's arduous chase, I have such fleetness
as would win the prize; — But all the pomps of circumstance
and place, A glance, a word, a smile of thine outvies! Leave
Fortune to her parasites! mine be The blessed lot to dwell
with love and thee. To lead thee on through life, and to en-
large Thy soul with added knowledge, day by day, To guard
thee, as an angel guards his charge, From every ill that lurks
along the way! To smooth that rugged way, and strew its
marge With the bright flowrs that never can decay, — This
were a lot too glorious, too divine, And yet Hope whispers
that it shall be mine. Now listen, love, — this plan shall rule
my life And thine: — In some remote and sunny dell, Far from
the crowded city's silly strife, My hands shall rear the home
where we will dwell; Shall till the soil, with fertile fruitage

rife, And teach the golden ear to shoot and swell; And my
sole wished for recompense shall be My ever growing,
deep'ning love for thee. Thy task shall be to train the trailing
vine, To watch, and cherish in its growth, the flow'r Whose
breath and cheek are sweet and fair as thine; To bless and
brighten the domestic bow'r Where we will build to Love a
hallowed shrine, And bow us, in his worship, every hour;
Till, chastened by thy smile, my heart has grown As pure,
and soft, and sinless as thine own. Oh, hasten, love! to realize
the dream, — Come from the world, — the crowd is not for
thee; Forsake it then, ere the contagious steam Of its foul
breath has soiled thy purity; — Come, for my heart would
burst could I but deem That such as they are, thou couldst
ever be! Come, for my soul adores thee with a love As burning as the seraphs feel above.

These lines are inscribed to the memory of John Q. Carlin, killed
at Buena Vista.

Warrior of the youthful brow, Eager heart and eagle eye!
Pants thy soul for battle now? Burns thy glance with victory?
Dost thou dream of conflicts done, Perils past and trophies
won? And a nation's grateful praise Given to thine after
days? Bloodless is thy cheek, and cold As the clay upon it
prest; And in many a slimy fold, Winds the grave-worm
round thy breast. Thou wilt join the fight no more, — Glory's
dream with thee is o'er, — And alike are now to thee Greatness and obscurity. But an ever sunny sky, O'er thy place of
rest is bending; And above thy grave, and nigh, Flowers ever
bright are blending. O'er thy dreamless, calm repose, Balmily
the south wind blows, — With the green turf on thy breast,
Rest thee, youthful warrior, rest! When the alarum first was
sounded, Marshalling in arms the brave, Forth thy fearless
spirit bounded, To obtain thee — what? A grave! Fame had
whispered in thine ear, Words the high-souled love to
hear, — But the ruthless hand of death From thee snatched
the hero's wreath. Often will the grief-shade start O'er thy sister's mood of joy, Vainly will thy mother's heart Yearn to
greet her absent boy; Never sister's lip shall press On thine

own its fond caress, — Never more a mother's eye Flash in
pride when thou art by! Where the orange, bending lowly
With its golden fruit, is swaying; And the Indian maiden,
slowly By her native stream is straying; O'er thy dreamless,
calm repose, Balmily the South wind blows, — With the green
turf on thy breast, Rest thee, youthful warrior, rest!

A LEGEND OF THE HARTZ.

Many ages ago, near the high Hartz, there dwelt A rude race
of blood-loving giants, who felt No joy but the fierce one
which Carnage bestows, When her foul lips are clogged with
the blood of her foes. And fiercer and bolder than all of the
rest Was Bohdo,(1) their chieftain; — 'twas strange that a
breast, Which nothing like kindness or pity might move,
Should glow with the warmth and the rapture of love. Yet he
loved, and the pale mountain-monarch's fair child Was the
maid of his heart; but tho' burning and wild Was the love
that he bore her, it won no return, And the flame that con-
sumed him was answered with scorn. Now the lady is gone
with her steed to the plain, — Save the falcon and hound
there is none in her train; She needs none to guide, or to
guard her from harm There's no fear in her heart, there is
strength in her arm. From her white wrist unhooded her falcon she threw, Her bow like Diana, the huntress, she drew;
And fleet as the fetterless bird swept the sky, So on her proud
steed swept the fair lady by. See how her eye sparkles, and
how her cheek glows, As onward so fearless and proudly she
goes, With her locks streaming back like a banner of gold,
Were she not, say, a bride meet for Nimrod(2) of old? And he
saw her — the chief, from his tower afar — As she glanced o'er
the earth like some wandering star; And he swore she should
come in that tower to dwell, Or his soul be a prize to the spirits of hell. His war-horse he mounted, and, swift as the shoot
Of the night-gathered meteor, he sped in pursuit, — Breath-

ing out, as he went, mad with love and with hate, Bitter curse upon curse against heaven and fate. Urging on his fleet courser with spur and with rein, He swept o'er the earth as the storm sweeps the plain, — And the fair lady knew, by the gleam of his shield, It was Bohdo, the scourge of the red battle field! Then spurred she her steed over valley and hill, Over rock, marsh and moor, over river and rill, Yet still her eye sparkled, and still her cheek glowed, As onward so fleetly and bravely she rode. Thus over Thuringia sped she away, With the speed of the hawk when he darts on his prey, — Or an arrow let loose from a warrior's bow, When it speeds with sure aim to the heart of his foe. Then the Hartz, the wild Hartz — the terrific — the proud! Where the mist-spirit dwells in his palace of cloud! Where the evil ones gather in envious wrath, To blight and to blast, — towered up in her path. Still her cheek kept its glow, still her eye flashed in pride, As onward she flew up the steep mountain side; And fierce as the tempest, and fleet as the wind, Stern Bohdo, the ruthless, still followed behind. To a fearful abyss, whose unhallowed name(3) By the powers of darkness was given, she came, And the whirlpool's wild voice, from the dark gulf below, Came up like the wail of a soul in its we. Beyond rose the rocky shelf, barren and bare, Beneath lay the whirlpool, around her despair, Behind her came one, sweeping on in the chase, Whose grasp was more dreaded than death's cold embrace. Then she called on the spirits who watch round the brave, In peril to nerve, to assist and to save, Closed calmly her eyes, as one sinking in sleep, And urged her proud steed to the terrible leap! A moment it paused on the high precipice, Then sprang, boldly sprang, o'er the frightful abyss! And struck its firm hoof in the rock till the sound Shook the hills, and the sparks flew like lightning around! And the footprint it left has remained to this day, And no rain-flood or tempest shall wear it away; She was saved — the brave Emma was saved — but her crown, From her fair brow unloosed, in the whirlpool sank down. On, on came the chief, in his fierceness and wrath, Nor saw he the wide gulf that yawned in his path, — And soon, in the depths of its fathomless tide, The warrior and war-steed were laid side by side. And the

mountaineer tells how in sullen despair, His ghost, iman-
nealed of its sins, lingers there; Ever watching, pale, silent,
untiring, unmoved, The bright golden crown of the maiden
he loved. A diver once, lured by the wealth of the prize,
Sought out the deep cave where it lay, and still lies, And
where, chained by a spirit-breathed spell, it shall stay, Till the
whirlpool and mountain alike pass away. Twice he rose with
the crown, till its gleaming points blazed On the eyes of the
wondering thousands who gazed, Twice it fell from his
grasp, and sank quickly again To the bed where for years
undisturbed it had lain. He followed, — this effort the treasure
may earn — But vainly they watch who await his return; A
red hue of blood tinged the deep waters o'er, But the diver
came up from their dark depths no more.

1. Bohdo. This hero, as his character is drawn in the original leg-
end, or tradition, from which the material of these verses was taken
(a tradition which gives the popular account of the formation of an
immense mark or cavity in a rock, called the "Rosstrappe" or
"Horse's footstep,") is worthy of being enrolled among Odin's Ber-
serker.

2. Nimrod. "A mighty hunter before the Lord." He built Babylon
and founded that royal line which terminated with the death of
Sardanapalus; whose gentleness and aversion to blood spilling,
together with his passion for his "Ionian Myrrha," cost him an empire, and gained him an immortality.

3. "It was named," says the tradition, "The Devil's dancing-place,
from the triumph there of the spirits of hell."